D0872200

Season of the Shadow

THE FRENCH LIST

Season of the Shadow

LÉONORA MIANO

Translated by Gila Walker

LONDON NEW YORK CALCUTTA

www.bibliofrance.in

The work is published with the support of the
Publication Assistance Programmes of the Institut français

Seagull Books, 2018

Originally published in French as *La Saison de l'ombre*, 2013

© Éditions Grasset & Fasquelle, 2013

English translation © Gila Walker, 2018

ISBN 978 0 8574 2 480 8

British Library Cataloguing-in-Publication Data
A catalogue record for this book is available from the British Library

Typeset by Seagull Books, Calcutta, India
Printed and bound by Hyam Enterprises, Calcutta, India

CONTENTS

To the shadow-dwellers
wrapped in the Atlantic shroud.
To those who loved them.

Watchman, what of the night?
Watchman, what of the night?
The watchman said,
The morning comes, and the night too.

Isaiah 21:11–12

Oh what future epic
will bring our vanished shadows back to life?

Frankétienne, *Ultravocal*

Fuliginous Dawn

They do not know it, but the thing comes to them at the same time. After several sleepless nights, the women whose sons went missing shut their eyes. Not all the huts have been rebuilt since the great fire. Grouped in a dwelling at a distance from the others, the women are fighting off their sorrow as best they can. All day long they say nothing of their anxiety, never utter the word loss or the names of their missing sons. In the absence of the spiritual guide, he too having disappeared no one knows where, the Council took the measures they deemed necessary. They summoned two women for advice, among the oldest of the clan. Two women who have not seen their blood for many moons. Women whom the clan now considers equal to men.

Of the two privileged to be consulted after the tragedy, particular consideration was given to Ebeise, the spiritual guide's first wife. As a midwife, she has assisted many women in childbirth. She has seen some of the dignitaries now seated on the Council trembling as they waited outside the hut where a life was coming to be, biting their lips, chewing on medicinal herbs to calm their nerves, praying to the maloba* to deliver them from the world of the living, so unbearable to them was the ordeal. She has seen them, hands pressed against their bellies, pacing back and forth, sweat dripping from their foreheads, as if they themselves were in labour.

She has seen them bragging when the newborn was presented to the manes. If the child was in the wrong position or, worse, if it was stillborn, she dried their tears, allayed their anxieties over the interminable series of sacrifices to be performed to ward off evil spirits. She is the one who prepared the herbal mix to be used when the parents of the stillborn were scarified. Here, a symbol is etched on the skin to remind death that it has already carried off a child of theirs. This woman has seen the sages fragile, lost. There is no one in the assembly of elders who can impress her.

Thus, she had the Council's ear. She was the one who suggested that the women whose children were missing be housed under the same roof. *In that way,* she declared, *their pain will be contained in a clearly defined place and will not spread throughout the village. We have much to do to understand what has happened to us, then begin rebuilding.* Careful not to be remiss, Mukano the chief, approving with a nod of his head the confinement of the grieving women, gave orders for the most valiant men to inspect the surrounding

---

* The reader will find a glossary of terms in Douala, one of the languages spoken on the Cameroonian coast, at the end of the volume.

bush. Clues might be found there to prevent other attacks.

Some Council members would have been inclined to level accusations. Point to failures with regard to the ancestors, the maloba or Nyambe Himself. What else could explain such a tragedy? The disgruntled swallowed their protests. It seemed wiser to them to show patience, leave their feeling unexpressed for the time being. Before releasing their arrows, they will wait for the damages to be repaired and thus avoid being blamed for opening the Council's door to the spirit of discord. Several times during the conversation, the midwife's unflinching gaze met the massive Mutango's. In the dignitary's big bulging eyes, she saw fury swelling, ready to pour forth upon the chief at the first opportunity. The two men are brothers by birth. Having come into the world nearly the same day but from different mothers, they both could have claimed the right to the chiefdom if the laws of the land had been different. But sovereignty among the Mulongo is passed down through the maternal line. Only Mukano's mother was of royal blood.

Mutango always felt this an injustice. He often drew attention to the incoherence on which the system was based. If women are considered children until they reach the age of menopause, it is absurd that they transmit this prerogative, even though it is the men who exercise supreme authority. Until now, the chief's brother has not succeeded in altering the rules, but in these troubled times he will surely manage to find allies to support him. Ebeise is wary of him. In the end, upon the Council's decision, a number of women from the community were gathered in the same hut. The women whose sons have not been found. Confinement was not deemed necessary for those who have not seen their husbands again. There are only two of them. The midwife and Eleke, the village healer, struck by a mysterious illness the day after the fire. She fainted as she was about to speak at the meeting of the elders. She had to be carried home. No one has seen her since.

*

The day is about to chase away the night on the lands of the Mulongo clan. The chorus of birds heralding the light has not been heard yet. The women are asleep. In their slumber, a strange thing is happening to them. As their spirit travels through the dream realms that are another dimension of reality, they have an encounter. A shadowy presence comes to them, to each one, and each one recognizes the distinctive voice that is speaking to her. As they dream, they lean forward, stretch their neck, try to peer into the shadow. To see this face. The darkness, however, is thick. They distinguish nothing. Nothing but these words: *Mother, open for me so I can be reborn.* They recoil. The voice insists: *Mother, hurry up. We have to act in front of the day. Otherwise, all will be lost.* Even with their eyes shut, the women know they ought to resist faceless voices. Evil exists. It knows how to pass itself off for what it is not. Day in and day out, their blood hungers for the being whose intonations they have now found. But what to do without certainty? A great misfortune has befallen the village. They refuse to be the cause of even more dreadful suffering. Already, they have been cast out, put at a distance from the group, as if they were evildoers.

To be sure, they were told that the measure was temporary—it was the midwife who explained it to them—that it would last only the time it took for the elders to make sense of the situation. Then they could go back home. This did not suffice to reassure them. They walk with their heads bowed. Speak little. Do not see their younger children left in the care of their co-wives. When it is time to lie down, they place their neck on a wooden headrest to keep their elaborate coiffure intact, hoping thereby to guarantee the quality of their dreams. The time dedicated for dreaming is approached with all the solemnity of a ritual. The dream is a journey both inside and outside the self, into the depths of things and beyond. It is not only a time but also a space. The site of an unveiling. At times of an illusion, for the invisible world is also peopled with evil entities. One does not rest one's head just anywhere when one is about to dream. An appropriate support is needed. An object carved from wood selected specifically for the spirit it harbours and over which sacred words have been pronounced before the carving begins. Even after taking all these precautions, it is not advisable to trust a voice that one thinks one has identified.

In a single movement, the women turn over. The gesture is nervous. They do not open their eyes. The voice becomes pressing, then vanishes. The final words echo in their minds: ... *in front of the day ... all will be lost.* Eyelids closed but tears flowing, they slip a hand between their legs, draw up their knees. They cannot open themselves like this. Let themselves be penetrated by a shadow. They weep. This happens to them all. Here, now. If one of them weakened, undid the lock, the others would know nothing. No one will speak of this dream. Not one will take a sister aside to whisper in her ear: *He came. My firstborn came. He asked me* ... They will not pronounce the names of their missing sons. Lest evil take hold of this particular vibration. If they are still alive, caution must be exercised. These names do not leave them. They sing within them from dawn to dusk, then pursue them into their sleep. Sometimes, they have nothing else in their mind. They will not utter them. They have already been isolated so that their heart's lament does not poison the lives of the others. The lucky ones who only lost a hut and a few things.

They open their eyes. Shortly before the birds sing the dawn. The shadow lingers, reluctant to dissipate. They feel like they are still dreaming, refrain from speaking, feign to sleep as they wait for day to break. Soon they tire of the pretence, cannot keep their eyes shut. Their gaze wanders in the darkness. Some think they can make out the patterns of the esoko mat on which they are lying, its crisscrossing fibres, the squares embroidered from slender leaf veins. They are motionless. Their necks still on the headrests. The mothers of the missing think for a moment that it is indeed fortunate that the master sculptor's hut was not destroyed completely. Some indispensable elements were rescued in time. For this reason, they do not have to roll up their mats to put under their heads and lie directly on the ground.

The light balks at taking its place. This they see through the open door. The door to the hut that was assigned to them does not close. They shiver imperceptibly as they wait for daybreak. Then they will go outside. Go about their business as if nothing happened. Wonder, without demanding anything, whether they will soon be authorized to return to their families. They will exchange commonplaces, nothing more. What people say when they are doing household chores. The words they speak when they are pounding tubers together. When collecting plant fibres to make a dibato or a manjua. Meanwhile, they wait. They peer into the darkness, inside and outside the communal hut. The women whose children went missing do not know that the sun has already taken up its quarters in the sky above. There it shines under the name of Etume, its first identity. In the course of the day, it will turn into Ntindi, Esama and Enange, marking the everyday course of time through its transformations.

Ebeise is the first to discover the phenomenon. She usually wakes up before dawn to prepare her spouse's meal. At sun-up, he only eats food cooked by his first wife. Today she will not be serving his breakfast. He too disappeared the night of the great fire. Now the clan is deprived of its spiritual guide.

Ebeise looks. Represses fear and anger, tries to understand. The thing is unprecedented. Discreetly, she leaves her hut to go to the home of her eldest son Musima. These days he sleeps under a tree at the rear of the family compound. When she reaches the spot, he is already up, burning bark while reciting incantations. He will go thereafter to put questions to the ancestors, set victuals at the foot of the reliquaries, cover his hands in oil to rub, with humility, their heads in carved wood. The disappearance of his father is inexplicable. A man like him does not simply vanish into thin air. Death itself could not have taken him by surprise. He would have seen it coming from afar. Known the exact moment. Left everything in order, well before the fatal encounter.

The son of the Minister of Rites and the midwife seems preoccupied. He is about to consult the ngambi one more time. His heart is not at peace. He feels weak because his father disappeared before teaching him all he needs to know. He has tried again and again to call his father to appear to him in his dreams, but he has not come. Once, he thought he heard his voice. It faded all too quickly. It was but a breath in the wind, a distant echo. Musima knows his father has the power, no matter where he is since the fire, to overcome distances. A spirit like his would not take so long to manifest itself, unless there was a cataclysm. And if he were no longer of this world, his son would have felt him entering him several days ago. At the sound of his mother's footsteps, Musima looks up. She signals to him not to say a word, to draw near. The woman has not performed her morning toilet. If she had, her skin would glisten with scented njabi oil. She would have powdered her face with red clay to protect it from the sun. The elder hastily slipped on her manjua, the clothing everyone has been wearing as a sign of lamentation since the great fire. They will remove it when reconstruction is completed. Then they will partake in the dindo, the meal marking the end of an ordeal. The matriarch wears no jewels. Only a pendant that never leaves her adorns her neck. The amulet swings between her naked breasts as she walks.

The man stands up, bows his head in a sign of respect. Ebeise whispers: *Son, come take a look at this. Quick, before everyone . . .* She pulls him by his arm. They do not have far to walk. The thing is visible from a distance. She points to the hut assigned to the women whose sons are missing. A thick fog hovers over the dwelling. Were such an oddity to exist, one could describe it as a cold smoke. This opacity prolongs the night around the hut while the sun has risen a few steps away. Mother and son look on. Breaking the silence, Musima stammers: *Do you think it is a manifestation of their pain?* She shrugs: *If we want to be sure, we have to ask them. And we should do so quickly before Mutango seizes the occasion to wreak havoc.* Their eyes meet again. Should they take a closer look? The fuliginous mass seems frozen over the hut, but it could well come crashing down on anyone who tries to examine it. They hesitate. After a few seconds, Ebeise decides to approach the place where the mothers of the missing are housed. Just then, a silhouette emerges from behind the hut in the distance. With her keen eyesight the matriarch recognizes the full figure of Mutango. *Sheesh*, she protests annoyed. *The fat man already knows. He may even have something to do with it. In any case, he must not see them before we do. Son, assume your responsibilities. In the absence of your father, you are the master of mysteries.*

Musima walks towards the dignitary with as much authority as he can muster, trying to keep his trembling legs under control. He does not feel ready to assume this role. It is not legitimate for him to do so as long as his father has not appeared to him in a dream. As long as his father's spirit has not descended upon him to transmit his knowledge before entering the other world. What should he do once he has reached the threshold of the hut? What question should he ask? To reassure himself, he caresses the talisman that has always hung from his neck, an object his father fashioned, to which he bestowed his power, with the help of the ancestors. His mother follows close behind. They are still at some distance from the place, when the notable looks up and sees them. Mutango knows he must not budge any more. Certainly he must not leave. Ebeise will not hesitate to call a meeting of the Council to place the blame on his shoulders. He waits. Seemingly unmoved by the darkness, though it hides the sky from his sight.

The midwife stops at the exact spot where day meets night. So does her son. Neither is in a hurry to meet the notable, who fixes his eyes upon her. The two size each other up wordlessly for a moment. Then, turning to her son, the woman whispers: *Get them out of the hut. Do not go inside. Call them.* The hut where the women are is far enough from most of the other dwellings. Musima can venture to raise his voice. He convokes the women residing under this roof, repeats their names like a litany. In the meantime, the matriarch and the dignitary continue to watch each other. They did not exchange the customary greeting and do not care. Their attitude is that of cardinal points, existing only in relation to each other, necessary to the balance of misipo and yet compelled not to touch, lest they cause the world to topple into chaos. Musima intones the names of the women whose sons are missing.

*

They cannot ignore this call. All of them hear it. Since they are no longer sleeping, it is not a dream. One of women, Eyabe, whispers: *You hear that?* The others nod silently. The one who spoke says: *We must not answer but we must find out if there is really someone outside.* It is dangerous to answer a call without knowing, with certainty, from whom it issues. It is best to go see. No one will go alone. Slowly they get up, gather at the centre of the room, wonder how to proceed so that no one will be more exposed than the others. *Let us close our eyes*, Eyabe suggests, *huddle together, take small steps to cross the threshold. When we are all outside, I will give the signal. We will open our eyes together.* Thus they will confront at the same time the person or spirit calling them so insistently.

The ten women hold one another. First two. Then a third joins them. Then a fourth. Until they form a cluster, like grains of njabi on the branches that bear them. They shut their eyes, bow their heads. Those were not the instructions but they do so spontaneously. The three rings of their cascading coiffures, multiplied by ten, form a wide corolla, with each level evoking a curved petal. Ever since their sons went missing, they have been but one and the same person. All of them surrounded by the same aura of mystery. Former rivalries have fallen away. Before, some would have refused to be thrown together so impetuously. Now the only thing that matters is not keeling over. They must keep pace. Truly be with the others. Espouse their movements. Anticipate them. Enter their breath. Breathe in and breathe out as one. Share sweat. The secret recollection of last night. They take their time.

Gripping one another, they share at last what words cannot say, since they must not utter these things. They embrace as one would cry. As one would dry a grieving friend's tears in the intimacy of one's home. Eyelids shut, they see one another, know one another, intensely. They take their time. Slow down to prolong the moment. They did not think of putting on their manjua. It is better this way, even though they are no longer of age to be entirely naked. Wives and mothers uncover their torso only. Outside, the voice is still calling them. The chant must not dictate the pace of their advance. The tempo must come from them. How long does it take to get out of the hut? They know they are outside when they feel a light breath of air on their skin and the roughness of the ground that has not been swept and smoothened like the ground inside the hut. Then, they stop. Eyabe murmurs a signal. They moan in unison, softly.

The women whose sons are missing need to cling to each other. Eyes shut. In silence. No one cares to console them. What the others are hoping is to ward off the misfortune that has befallen these women. If their sons are never found, if the ngambi does not reveal what happened to them, no one will speak of their distress. The community will forget the ten young initiates and the two older men who vanished during the great fire. Nothing will be said of the fire itself. Who wants to relive the memory of a defeat? The people now know it was no accident. The village was attacked. And the power of the ancestors, the skill of the older warriors, the agility of the young fighters did not prevent it from happening. Eyabe murmurs the signal. They moan. When they open their eyes, night has undone the veils that surrounded the hut. The morning bird sings its song. The young master of mysteries falls silent. Without a word, the midwife and the notable shoot flaming arrows at each other. It is as if they sought to destroy each other with their gaze. They have no eyes for the women who know not whether to cry or to wait. They stand there, silent, naked, and slowly separate. Each one is alone again. The sun lodges its radiance in the sky. They have never felt so cold.

*

The matriarch's son addresses the women: *We must talk.* He does not ask them about the strange way they had of coming out, sticking fast to one another, eyes shut, heads bowed. The man says they will each speak in turn. Since they are not permitted to circulate in the village, he will stay here with them. He gestures to his mother and Mutango to go away. The notable does not budge. Calmly Musima explains: *In the absence of my father, it is my role to do this. I am ready.* He does not really think so but this is what he must say. His mother nods in approval. The elders turn their back on him and walk away in opposite directions.

The man has the women sit down in front of the hut, in a row. He intends to keep an eye on them. While speaking with one, he will make sure that the others do not say anything to one another. Each woman must deliver her truth. They all accept the principle. They have been living apart from the others for more than three weeks now. No one has wanted to hear what weighs on their hearts, what every woman keeps to herself. Good manners prohibit outbursts of emotion. One is not supposed to moan over the fate of a child when there is a chance of having others, when one can still give birth. It is immoral to indulge in one's own suffering when what matters is the continued existence of the group. It is common knowledge that they are in pain. It is why they were assigned to this communal dwelling.

They have the right to experience grief but not to embarrass the clan with all their woe, to contaminate the people who live by their side every day, to act as if the missing child represented everything. These women are like widows who are authorized to reappear in public only after a period of time, after submitting to sometimes gruelling rituals. But they are not widows. There is no name for their condition. Their sons have not been seen since the great fire. Nobody knows if they are dead or alive.

*

Musima starts interviewing them. He improvises, persuades himself that he has chosen an appropriate procedure. He asks each one the same questions. They take turns answering. *Woman, how did you leave the night?—Well, thank you.—Woman, what have you to say about the shadow?* Every one of them has the same reaction to this question. They look at him fixedly for a long time, sure he knows the content of the dream that assailed them. They stammer: *Mwititi . . . —Woman, what have you to say about the shadow?* Nine out of the ten women reply: *Mwititi is deceitful. She came to me, speaking in the voice of my eldest son. The one who is missing. I know it was not him.* Then they fall silent. They have said too much. It is hard to weigh one's words when the right to voice thoughts has been taken away. They let them brim over.

One alone replies: *The shadow is all we have left. It is what the days have become.* Eyabe is the one who speaks these words. She adds: *And you, man, what have you to say of Mwititi? Do you believe that all it takes is to relegate ten women to a corner of the village for the community to be safe?* Eyabe meets Musima's baffled gaze and gets up without waiting for him to give her leave. Not once did she lower her head. Instead of joining her companions sitting in front of the hut, she walks behind it. She returns washed, a crown of leaves on her head, her face and shoulders covered in kaolin. The other women shudder at the sight. The man stifles a cry. White clay, applied to the face, symbolizes the figure of the deceased who come to visit the living. White is the colour of spirits. Without paying the slightest attention to anyone, Eyabe steps inside the hut. She hums a lament, softly claps her hands.

She soon comes back out wearing a dibato in barkcloth. It is ceremonial dress, not like the manjua. Slowly, Eyabe walks towards the village centre. Every step is an affirmation. She has done nothing wrong. First, she utters these words to herself. Then she says them aloud, without shouting, includes the other women in the denial: *We have done nothing wrong. We have not swallowed our children and we do not deserve to be treated like criminals. What was needed was to search for them. By now, they are no longer. As we knew them, we will not see them again . . .* Her voice breaks, but she walks on, clapping her hands to give rhythm to her chant, approaches a first group of huts, passes without stopping. Eyabe reaches her family compound. Since the Council decided to isolate the women whose children are missing, no one has tried to see her.

Someone extends a half-hearted greeting. She ignores it, seems not to hear, walks around her hut. In a small courtyard, in the rear, are trees. Makube. One of them was planted the day her son came into the world. The one who is missing. The one about whom she is not supposed to speak. The dead are constantly referred to in the Mulongo community. The living are the subject of incessant gossip, sometimes of praise. But ever since the great fire, a new category of individual has emerged: they are neither alive nor dead. No one knows what happened to them. People accept living without knowing. Eyabe huddles against the dikube beneath which the placenta was buried the day she gave birth to her first son who was stolen from her on the threshold of adulthood. *Where you are*, she says, *will you hear my heart calling you? I know you suffered. You came to me in my dream yesterday. Forgive me for not understanding right away. Come back and I will open myself up and shelter you again.*

Eyabe speaks to her son without opening her mouth. The inhabitants of the compound watch her, say she has lost her senses, see her rub her forehead against the tree, caress it. The woman cries. She grants herself the right to do so. In the end, she steps away from the dikube, withdraws without taking her eyes off of it. The tree falls, as if torn from the earth by a powerful hand. The roots are visible as is the trough they left in the ground. Eyabe is the only one to know that the hole contains a plant. A flower unlike any she has seen before. A tiny flower that a child would present to his mother to show her the beauty of things. Beauty, in spite of all, for sorrow cannot erase what has been lived, the love that has been given and received, shared joys, memories. The woman dries her tears and starts singing again. Bending forward, she performs the dance of the dead, stamping her bare feet on the ochre earth, until she reaches the threshold of her hut and sets foot inside.

All that remains of her dwelling are the pillars, half a roof, one wall and part of another. No matter. Eyabe will not wait for directives from the elders to regain possession of her space, of her life. Once inside, she takes the lende leaf fibres, bundled and attached together to form a broom, and sweeps the floor of her hut. She unrolls the mat she herself plaited, spreads it out on the floor. Along the only still-intact wall, the one against which the rolled mat was placed, stands a vertical column of clay pots containing her personal affairs. She repositions them, sets a few on the ground until she finds the one she is seeking. Smoke from the fire covered the pots with the soot that now blackens the palm of her hands. Looking at her dirty fingers, she murmurs, *Woman, what have you to say about the shadow? It suffices to open one's eyes to know what to make of this . . .* Eyabe puts her dibato made of dikube barkcloth into a large, empty pot. She wore it to address the spirit of her son, the one . . . whom she will never see as she once knew him. She will not wear this garment again.

She is being watched. Most of the interior of the hut is visible from outside. The compound's inhabitants, her relatives, are standing there without moving, staring as if she were a stranger. From time to time, they exchange a few words in a low voice. She leans against the half-wall that gives onto the remains of the neighbouring hut, the dwelling of her co-wife Ekesi, who looks daggers at her. Eyabe returns her co-wife's affection: *I am surprised, my dear, that you are still here looking at me. What are you waiting for before alerting the Council and demanding a trial by ordeal?* And turning to the crowd of curious spectators in the courtyard, Eyabe adds: *No one need have fear of me. After all,* she goes on with a faint smile, *I have not suddenly become evil.* She would like to say more, to plead the case of the women whose first sons are missing. It is pointless. She sees this, she feels it. The family does not want her to come back. The women, alone in their compound with their younger children, cross their arms over their chests in a defensive posture.

Without understanding, the little ones sense the thickening tension in the atmosphere. Some cry. Fear is reflected in the onlookers' eyes, as if her presence alone could spark a new fire, could make others disappear. Musinga, her husband, must be somewhere in or around the village, in charge of a mission with which the chief entrusted him. If he were here, would his attitude be different? Would he take her defence? They were together the night of the great fire. It was Ekesi's turn but he made believe he had forgotten. When she tried to make him to listen to reason, he insisted: *You know I do not love her. I only married her to please my parents . . . Must we really talk about it? It is when I am with you that my heart is at rest.* This great love did not bring the man to show his support for her. Otherwise he would have defied the prohibition, would have come to see her in the communal hut, at least once. He did not do so. Eyabe has just come to a decision. She will say nothing to him either.

*

The janea, the midwife and her son are sitting under the tree called buma. It is a colossus with a thick bark and a huge trunk that is older than all the other trees growing in these parts. Its foliage provides shelter from the sun. The three are waiting for the members of the Council. The disappearance of the Minister of Rites complicates the situation. The chief possesses some of the clan's mystical powers but he is not authorized to replace the occult mediator. Mukano chews pensively on a root with mind-illuminating virtues. He has admitted to no one that he has absorbed these fibres in such great quantities since the night of the fire that his entrails are saturated with them. That night, from the hilltop where the chiefdom is built, he and the others from his compound watched the sudden blaze engulfing the village. By the time they came down, there was nothing they could do.

The man relives these moments, sees himself leaping from his bed at the sound of the uproar from the village. Flames. Everywhere. Screaming. He rushes to his brother's compound and surprises the doings of the huge notable with a girl so young she had not seen her blood yet. The child cries, hides her face from the chief. She murmurs: *Sango janea, forgive me. He left me no choice.* She trembles with shame. With fear. Even though she was unwilling, she fears she is guilty of a transgression and will be punished by the Council for it. The chief studies her, sees she is one of Mutango's daughters. A child born from his loins who, even if she were not so young, has no business being there. Mukano roars: *You are an animal. We will see about this later. Come quickly, the village is on fire.*

Mukano realizes that he has neglected to bring his brother before the Council because of the great fire. Given his brother's rank, the assembly is not likely to sentence him to banishment, the requisite punishment for such a deed. Nonetheless, he must be chastised. The girl will have to testify. Will she have the courage? Mutango's guards will surely not talk. They are too afraid of their master. The roots the janea is chewing should be consumed in moderation. Yet he has no peace of mind, no more than do his subjects. The fire, whatever its cause, is a dark omen, a presage of torments for the clan. He wonders at times what purpose it serves to exercise this function.

His decisions must be approved by at least half the Council members.

Since the fire, Mukano has not succeeded in convincing them to adopt the only measure he deems pressing, more so than rebuilding the village. The chief would have liked not to confine the community's warriors to finding evidence to explain the event. His inclination was to send them out beyond the immediate vicinity of the village, to the Bwele people, to the end of the world if necessary. He thought that everything should be done to find the missing. That the ancestors, whose sole ambition was to see their descendants prosper, not be abandoned through these abducted sons. Notwithstanding their certainty by the very next day that the fire was no accident, the members of the Council would hear nothing of it. The janea suspects his brother of filling their heads with mystical ideas, when what happened is clearly the work of men. Men who must be punished for their crimes. *I am because we are*—this has been the clan's motto since its origin. For the first time, Mukano has the feeling he has violated this dictum by not managing to impose his will. For him, not attempting to find the missing, as impossible as the task may turn out to be, amounts to surrendering a piece of himself to the abyss.

Three weeks have elapsed. Today, more than ever, he needs to ingest this root purported to bestow clairvoyance. He plans to disregard the feckless Council, to set out on the road with his personal guards. That way, he will not be accused of dragging into a risky enterprise warriors whose function it is to serve the entire community. Yes, he will travel every path, do everything in his power to bring back the missing sons. The janea swallows the bitter juice of the roots, spits out the fibres, watches the wind cover them with red dust. His two companions, as silent as stones, have the glum mien of those who have crossed paths, first thing in the morning, with the shadow of a bad spirit freshly returned from his evil doings. Mukano begins to weary of waiting. Just as he is about to open the session despite the absence of members of the Council, they arrive.

The elders are in no hurry. They have evidently met before coming to him, since they show up together. Only Mutango is not there, which is not surprising. The chief has the sense that he has made a mistake in not gathering the information that the midwife and her son wanted to bring to the attention of Council. After all these years, he still imagines that honesty and uprightness are superior values. Subterfuge is not his strength. He does not allow himself any breach of morality, does not practise dissimulation. Owing to his irreproachable behaviour, he has not been removed from his functions, despite his brother's incessant scheming. After the customary greetings, the meeting is called to order. Mukano takes the floor: *I summoned you, brothers, because Musima and his mother have something to tell us. As you may imagine, it is about the ten whose sons are missing.* The chief turns to the apprentice Minister of Rites: *We are listening.*

Musima's throat is dry. His chest is so tight from anxiety that the sounds he utters resemble a frail wheezing. He speaks of the thick veil that clouded the rays of the dawning day. The members of the Council shudder when they hear that the phenomenon occurred over the communal hut only. So he questioned its occupants. He asked each of them: *Woman, what have you to say about the shadow?* Nine women out of the ten gave the same answer. Only Eyabe, the last to be questioned, dared ask him what he had to say about Mwititi. Mukano urges him to tell them more about what the women said. The new Minister of Rites repeats what he heard word for word. The Council members are speechless. The whole business is a mystery. Ebeise profits from their dismay to speak her mind. *I think*, she declares, *that we should not let appearances fool us and rush to incriminate Eyabe simply because she alone had something personal to say.* The midwife knows what happens when the Council finds no solutions. They choose the most expedient solution. Experience demonstrates that truth is more complex than it appears.

None of the women whose sons are missing are guilty of any wrongdoing, she insists. She chooses her words carefully in the hope that the notables will not pass sentence lightly. One of them replies: *Woman, it is only natural that you defend your sisters but your empathy will not suffice to convince us. What do you have to say about the ring of darkness that surrounded the communal hut?* He reminds her that if it were not for her prudent advice, the ten women would have gone home to their family compounds after the great fire. *You did well in urging us to remove them from the community since events have demonstrated that they were indeed bearers of malefic energies.* The midwife does not know what to say about the dark veil she saw at the break of day. Her intuition prompts her to do all she can to ensure that the grieving mothers are not accused of witchcraft and banished from the clan. Such is the sentence when neither the mind nor the heart can find a way to be reassured. The person who is cast out is provided with a hand of makube, a gourd filled with water. In silence, a signal is given for the person to leave. To go as far as possible from the clan's lands. This is the procedure. It has not been applied since time out of mind. Otherwise they would already have sent Mutango away. Ebeise feels a shudder running through her at the thought that the women whose children are missing could be sent out into the bush and beyond where no one has ever ventured before. She will not allow this to happen.

Her voice resonates with authority. *It is simple. They are thinking so hard about their children that they thought they saw them in their dreams. And the pain is so intense that the dreams took the form of a cloud. That is how I explain the shadow. After all*, she adds, *we do not know how our thoughts materialize when we sleep. We saw it for the first time today because the women were all in the same place and there has never been such a situation before.* She stops there. The chief nods thoughtfully and asks Musima what he recommends. The midwife's son clears his throat, strains to get his dry tongue moving. In a near whisper, he recommends that the nine women who gave the same response to his question undergo a ritual of purification. Without lifting his eyes towards his mother who he can feel stiffening by his side, he continues: *I am sorry, iyo, but I do not share your opinion about Eyabe̲. I found her attitude very disturbing . . .*

We are all disconcerted, the midwife replies more vehemently than she would have liked. *Twelve men from our village disappeared after an attack. We are suffering, but we must not be blinded by our emotions. Everyone here knows that Eyabe̲ has a character all her own, that she walks to the beat of a different drum. Are we going to condemn her for that? Now is the time to remember the principles that have always governed us and take care of one another instead of assigning guilt to individuals in our midst.* After this tirade, Ebeise̲ tries to calm herself, reminds all present of the danger of knowingly committing an injustice. *It is not our daughter who started the fire that has left so many villagers without a roof over their heads. We must hold those who did so accountable instead of resorting to who-knows-what rituals of purification.*

A mother's sorrow is not a taint. It is noble, especially among our people since it is motherhood that confers an honourable status on women. Our men are glad to marry a woman who already has a child. Then they are sure of her fertility. When I asked that our sisters and daughters not be authorized to return immediately to their family homes, it was also because of the shock they received. Out of respect. How could they have shared their husbands' bed, *argued with their co-wives, taken care of the other children in their families when they had just learnt that their firstborns were gone.* In the communal hut, they *could collect their thoughts, say things to one another they alone could understand.* I hope, the midwife murmurs, *they are talking to one another. The shadow is also the shape our silences take.*

These last words Ebeise keeps to herself. They echo in her mind as if they harboured a secret message. Yes, Mwititi is the shape silences take. The thing is true, at least for four members of the Council. Since the start of the discussion, they have not opened their mouths. You can hardly hear them breathe. After gathering at Mutango's at dawn, they thought they would see him again here, under the buma. They left his dwelling, picked up a fifth man, then headed to the meeting place. The voice of the fat dignitary is missing from the discussion. No one dares utter the words he pronounced. *Only a trial by ordeal will tell us if the shadow was conjured by the women whose sons are missing.*

The discussions seem deadlocked. The midwife feels suddenly very old. Since the fire, she has not taken the time to dwell on her own fears as to her husband's fate. Ebeise is tired of being a pillar of strength. Just as she is about to ask permission to leave the meeting, a young boy appears, with a message that he refuses to communicate to the guards. The child announces that Eyabe has returned to her family compound. The voice of the janea is heard. He addresses the midwife: *Woman, bring her to me. I want to speak to her.* He beckons to the servant who always awaits his instructions, directs him in a whisper to go look for Musinga, his best detective: *Tell him I want to know where my brother is. Have him report to me here.*

*

In front of the communal hut, the women whose sons are missing are deep in discussion. Eyabe's conduct has them wondering. Some of the women would like to go back to their homes like she did. It is not by staying cloistered in this hut that they will have a chance of seeing their sons again. The midwife, who usually reports on Council discussions, barely approached them. Only on the day they moved into the communal hut was she there to give them instructions:

You will draw water every other day, as we always do, but you will wait until your sisters from the village have returned from the source. You will get your food from the field behind your hut. You will cultivate this land like all the women of our community do. You will eat no meat while you are living here. Everything you will need is here. One of my co-wives has gathered fabric and fibres for you to make your clothes and mats.

The matriarch was careful to give these directives from a good distance, as if she were speaking to strangers encountered unexpectedly on a road. While the life of the clan returns to normal, the women whose sons are missing have no idea what the clan intends to do to find out what happened to their firstborns. As they speak to each other for the first time, their eyes turn to the village that they have avoided contemplating, even from afar, until now. The days after the fire, when it was decided they would be separated from the others, they took to thinking they deserved punishment. The disappearance of their sons could not be a coincidence. They must have been guilty of something, even unwittingly.

No one told them the communal hut was meant to contain their sorrow until it was clear that their bereavement, once subjugated, would not be transmitted to the other families. No one suggested to the women whose sons were missing that they might sing and dance their grief, the better to rise above it. Even though this was the tradition. No one told them whether they could cry. Tears are reserved for those whose loved ones have been seen lying lifeless. They were left with nothing but silence and solitude. They were left with nothing but this absence to which no words of mourning can be addressed, words that express the acceptance before opening a passage to the other world: *Nyambe alone is master of these things. I have no power. Son, may your passage be peaceful. Son, may the ancestors guide you for they know all your names, all your faces.*

Silence. Solitude. Absence. Clutching them like a stranglehold. They did not know what to do, how to loosen its grip. They watched the women of the clan go to the source, escorted by the warriors. Afterwards, they too went to draw water from the source. No one accompanied them. At no time, when they went out, did it occur to them to run away. Where would they go? Women do not roam the countryside alone. Women embody the permanence of things. They are the pillar that holds up the hut. Today they are talking to each other, speaking of how heavy their hearts felt seeing their friends and sisters pass by on their way to the water source without saying a word. Nobody misses them. Life goes on without them. Their children have other mothers. Their men, other companions to embrace. The women whose sons are missing know they will not be supported if they return on their own initiative to their homes.

The sun is high in the sky. They did not notice time passing by. They have had nothing to eat or drink since the chanting that drew them out of the hut. But they are not hungry. They fall silent. Each one sinks down into herself to the place where the shadow has left its mark. The place where the voice heard in their sleep continues to resonate. Ebusi breaks the silence: *I am going to see Eyabe. And, if I have the courage, I am going back to my family*, she announces. The women whose sons are missing are like a fabric unravelling little by little. Their solidarity was but a semblance. Each one is grappling with her own thoughts, her own emotions. Each one has a particular relationship with the departed son, rooted in the circumstances of his birth. Was the child born of violence or of love? Did he see the light of day after strangling his twin in his mother's womb? Did roosters have to be sacrificed before presenting him to his forefathers because he did not cry out or was born from a breech presentation? In each case the mother's attitude is different. Yet they are all here. Naked, distraught. Regardless of whether they are hoping for the return of their beloved sons or see the disappearance of the painfully born offspring as the hand of immanent justice.

The mothers who would have opened the door to their son, refrained from doing so because of the darkness that covered his face. They were not sure it was him. The others would not have accepted, in any case, to welcome this son into their womb again. They all did the same thing: they pressed their knees against their chests and slipped their arms between their legs to prevent access. What keeps them from speaking of this too? Ebusi does not hesitate for long. Getting up to seek out Eyabe, she confides: *Last night, I had a dream. Someone came to see me. It was all so dark that I could not see his face. But I clearly recognized my firstborn's voice. He wanted something. I could not hear him. He seemed so weak . . .*

Ebusi speaks her mind. She left the night trembling. Her intuition tells her that her son has suffered unimaginable torments. Has she demonstrated poor judgement? As she walks to the rear of the hut, she explains: *My son may have left this life but of this I am not sure. All I can do now is ask the ancestors to protect him.* Indifferent to the reaction of her companions, she disappears behind the hut. The others lend an ear. Sounds of water reach them. The woman is washing up. Will she come back with her face covered in white clay, like Eyabe? They shudder at the thought.

*

Ebeise walks with heavy steps, her progress slowed by the weight of her worries. She wonders whether she has made the right decisions, whether she behaved well towards the women whose sons are missing. She is wracked with doubt. Finally, she decides not to go to Eyabe's. She must speak to someone. She has only one friend, chides herself for not having gone sooner to ask for advice from the only person who is capable of hearing her. The only other woman to sit on the Council. The woman whose husband also went missing after the great fire. They have known each other from as far back as either can remember. They were initiated together. They married the same year. They gave birth to their first sons a few days apart.

As she walks, Ebeise looks around her. Here and there the red earth is still streaked with black. No matter how often the women have swept over the past three weeks, they cannot erase the marks of the disaster. Just a few huts have been rebuilt out of the five or six that each family compound possesses. There are no fences around the homes. Near the door, an excavation conferring the appearance of a cavern on the clan's dwellings, a carved wood pillar is placed that represents the family totem. There are no totems, no protection near the entrance to the huts that are being rebuilt. The midwife sighs at the sight of such desolation. It is unthinkable that such a thing has happened. And yet there it is. The clay huts with their thatched roofs, at all events those that have not been burnt to the ground, are covered with long charred stains. It was decided not to rebuild them so close together in the future. The proximity allowed the fire to spread more quickly—it sufficed to set one roof on fire, and the roof next door erupted in flames too.

At least it is not raining. The villagers can put up with sleeping under the stars for some time still. An attack of this kind could not have happened during the rainy season when the Mulongo are isolated. Then the roads to Bwele territory are hardly passable and there is less trade between the two communities. The midwife has heard talk of other populations but she does not know them. One would probably have to travel great distances through the heart of the bush to reach the lands of these unknown clans. She has never had the opportunity to undertake such a voyage and learn something of the strangers that may have set fire to the village. For Ebeise, like for all Mulongo living in our time, the world is limited to the lands of her people and to those of the Bwele. She saw the Bwele's territory only once and that was long ago.

She and her best friend, then new initiates, had thirsted for adventure. Even today, they both agree that too many prohibitions are imposed on women, on the pretext that they have been endowed with the great privilege of giving life and transmitting the power to rule. They are not allowed to explore the countryside. Acquiring knowledge of the world is not permitted. Yet, during their initiation, their elders told them the history of the clan, spoke rhapsodically of Queen Emene who led her people to the place that has become their territory so as to prevent a massacre. The princess had been designated by her father to be his successor. Where she came from, the throne went to the ruler's firstborn, male or female. A pretender to the throne could not be disqualified unless he or she demonstrated incompetence or was guilty of some infamous act. Emene's behaviour was above reproach. So before he departed this world, the king gave her the staff of authority.

Her brother, whose name was Muduru, had no intention of accepting this. Long in advance he prepared his coup, gained the allegiance of a good number of notables by promising them the moon in exchange for their support. And so it was that, in the early days of her reign, Emene saw her people divided, ready to kill each other. Never before had disagreements taken such a tragic turn. Clashes in the community would be played out in rituals without physical violence: verbal jousts, danced fights and games of intellectual skill. Weapons were used for hunting or as objects of prestige and symbols of power. But now Muduru and his followers were threatening to take human lives. There were as many people who remained faithful to the young queen because they knew her value and respected her father's word, beyond death, as those who stood behind her brother.

At first, the sovereign dismissed the very idea of capitulation. The staff of command deserved to be defended so it would not fall into evil hands. If Muduru wanted war, he would have it. She was ready. She had proven herself many a time in hunting as in other areas. She was not afraid of dying. Death was a continuation of life. Nothing more than an alteration in the vibration of beings. As she was preparing for the fight, the spirit of the king, her father, came to her and changed her mind. He reminded her that it was the tradition in cases of serious conflict for one of the two warring parties to leave the land. Nothing can flourish, nothing solid can be built if it requires stepping over the dead bodies of one's own people to make it happen. This is how the exodus began.

The nation split in two and the queen's partisans chose to follow her. They walked. A long way. To grasp what it means to have hope and faith in life, just picture Emene leading her people. The elders telling the story could not measure the distance travelled, so they named the cardinal points to express the immensity of space that had to be put between the prince's supporters and his sister's. They said: *They walked and walked and walked. From pongo to mikondo where we live today. They walked, my children, oh how they walked, until the sole of their feet wedded the ground. Until they simply could not take another step.* The midwife remembered these words as if she had heard them yesterday. Sitting huddled together in the hut where the girls of her age group had been gathered, she and her friend listened, eager for details about Queen Emene.

They asked questions, each in turn and then in chorus: *So our people come from pongo? What was the name of the land of origin? Why mikondo? Why not jedu or mbenge? And, auntie, can you tell us if they met anyone on their way? Was there not a living soul over such a great distance? And where did the Bwele, our neighbours, come from? What is the story of their migration? Their territory is said to be vast . . . Where does it end?* Some of these questions had answers. Most did not. At least not officially. Ebeise and this friend who was closer to her than a sister took to fantasizing about their clan's courageous founder. The status of women changed when Her Majesty Emene departed to the land of the dead. When her firstborn son Mulongo received the staff of command several generations ago, he decreed that the seat and staff of authority would be transmitted from mother to son. And men could take several wives if they so desired.

The name of this queen from the past is no longer mentioned save in the teachings imparted to girls during initiation. If ever a reliquary was sculpted in her honour, it is not revered. The statue affixed to the cavity containing her mortal remains is never anointed with love and respect. Her spirit seldom receives offerings. Women who are said to be possessed by a virile force sometimes secretly invoke the forgotten sovereign when they are about to face a difficulty. They call out: *Emene, you who walked from pongo to mikondo to give your people a land, please help me.* One day in their youth, Ebeise and Eleke were out gathering herbs in the bush when they caught sight of a group of men from their clan heading to Bwele territory. They followed them, hid behind shrubs and trees, holding their breath. When the men stopped for the night, the girls did too.

The teenagers were discovered the next day at dawn as the convoy was about to reach its destination. They were told they would be punished, but in the meantime they saw part of Bekombo, the capital of Bwele country. The dwellings were spacious; they were not circular; their roofs were made of earth, not leaves. Carved wooden doors closed the entrance to the homes. On the outer walls, friezes were painted representing the household's totem, conveying a message or relating an important event. The Bwele women painted the friezes with rock soaked in white clay and in a plant decoction that yielded a dark colour.

Whereas three or four households in a Mulongo compound would share a single granary, here every dwelling was flanked by one of its own. The two young adventurers were instructed to wait on the outskirts of the great Bwele city while the men went to trade. They had nonetheless seen these things and watched dumbfounded as the men of their tribe negotiated with the Bwele women. No woman from their community had ever walked this far. When they related what they had seen, their sisters accused them of exaggerating to make themselves seem interesting. Their punishment was several days of domestic work for the boys of their age group; they escaped corporal punishment due to Eleke's noble descent. The midwife smiled at the memory of those days.

She climbs with small steps the hill where her friend lives. The ascent seems to take for ever. The landscape around her changes. No burnt huts here. Deciduous trees spread their branches over imposing dwellings. The ruling family members have been spared. Their totems, still in place, rise proudly to the sky. Ebeise feels a burning in her thighs and shooting pains in her calves as she climbs. She is out of breath. A trickle of sweat drips down her back between her shoulder blades. Soon she reaches the compound neighbouring the chief's. Posted at the entrance are guards wearing a headdress of plant fibre that calls to mind a lion's mane. Recognizing her, they bow their heads, step aside with a greeting: *Our aunt, how did you leave the night?* She replies with a nod of the head.

Now, standing in front of one of the huts, Ebeise calls out: *Eleke ooo . . . Your sister is here to see you. Please forgive me for taking so long. May I come in?* Immediately a young woman comes out, lowers her eyes, greets her. Yes, she is welcome. Her friend has been waiting for her for a long time but she holds nothing against her. The midwife steps through the door into a single circular room. As in all huts occupied by women, jars of personal belongings are piled up along the walls. The cooking is done outside, but the utensils, calabashes, mortars and pestles are kept inside. In a terracotta cup, a fragrant bark resin, known for its air-purifying qualities, melts slowly under the heat of coals. Eleke is lying feverish, on her mat. She cannot get up. One of her daughters-in-law—the young woman who came out to welcome Ebeise—is caring for her.

The midwife feels all her joints creaking as she crouches to sit down beside the mat. Gently she touches her friend's forehead and whispers: *Eleke, this illness will not let go? If Mundene had been here, he would have rid you of it long ago.* After uttering these words, she falls silent. The tingling at the rims of her eyes tells her she is about the break down and cry. In a rather hoarse voice, the sick woman addresses her daughter-in-law: *Go now to prepare a little bopolopolo for me. You know I need to take some regularly. Also go to Aunt Elokan. Ask if she still has any akene . . .* The young woman understands; she leaves her elders. As soon as she walks out, the midwife lets her tears flow. Her friend takes her hand: *Daughter of Emene, what have you done with your strength?*—*Ah, my sister,* Ebeise replies, *the power of our mother deserted me long ago. I wonder about my decisions. And then, there is the disappearance of my husband. He has not manifested himself to me or to my elder son. Something is not right. I am afraid . . .*

Only Eleke can hear the midwife utter such words. In front of no one else would Ebeise allow herself to behave like an ordinary person, beset by anxieties and fear of failure. *Ebeise,* says the sick woman, *you have every reason to be afraid. Something very serious has happened.* Her hand in her friend's, little by little, Ebeise calms down. Everything seems clearer to her. With the women whose sons are missing, she should have done things differently. With humility, she relates the events of recent weeks. The sick woman sighs: *Do not be so hard on yourself. It is not easy to always do the right thing when you can rely on no one but yourself. And those old scoundrels are of no help, this we both know, when it comes to serious matters. I am the one who regrets that I could not help you.* Eleke talks about the nature of the fever that took hold of her the day after the fire. It is not an ordinary illness that you can treat by taking bopolopolo to cleanse the blood. As the clan's established healer, she would have easily cured a simple disease. She would need to consult the spiritual guide but he is gone. Eleke has been wrestling with visions that have assailed her ever since the twelve clansmen went missing. One of them, Mutimbo, is her husband. She married him because he had been the choice of heart. And he had accepted not to take another woman in order to be united with her.

Unlike Eleke, he was not of noble extraction. He could not have provided for the high-ranking women he would have been required to marry if he had opted for polygamy. It was inconceivable in Mulongo society to devalue a woman of a prestigious lineage by giving her co-wives of a lower status. When they married, Mutimbo left his family compound to settle on the hillside where his chosen lived. He had faced the mockery and humiliation from his in-laws to which young married women are usually subjected. This is the man whom Eleke misses. The day after the fire, she realized he was gone. What happened when the fire spread? In which direction did Mutimbo go?

Why does she believe him to be wounded. She does not know. All she knows is that he has been gone for three weeks and that she has been visited by faceless utterances. Everyone thinks the old woman is delirious. Yet she is simply repeating, in a low voice with her fever-dried trembling lips, the words of the bodiless speaker. Often these words make no sense. The woman repeats them as they come to her but she cannot always hear distinctly. At such times, she moans and groans, and insists on knowing what happened to her husband, to her dear beloved.

Now having deciphered the messages, she affirms that the Bwele have the answer to the questions the Mulongo are asking. They know what became of the missing. This is what the voice, muffled as it is, repeats incessantly. *It is time*, she declares, *for our chief to present himself in person before the queen of our neighbours. Take him aside to tell him. I do not trust his brother's minions.* As for the women in the communal hut, Elke sees that the midwife has grasped her error. It will not be easy to fix but she can gain some time. *Do not abandon them. Insist that a delegation be sent to the Bwele before the fate of our girls is decided. It is unacceptable to subject them to a ritual of purification when they have done nothing to warrant cleansing. There are other measures to take. Hurry. After all these days of solitude, the women will start to falter. Discord will take hold.*

Eleke coughs. A long fit of hacking shakes her body so violently her friend has to hold her with both hands to keep her from rolling across the room. She is burning up, her lips are cracked, her eyes yellow. She seems not to be eating much. She complains of a dreadful pain in her groin, but nothing can be done to help her for there is no wound, not the slightest scratch. The two old women stay together a moment longer but Ebeise has much to do. The chief wants to see Eyabe. She must fetch the woman and use the occasion to tell the janea what her friend has said. Then she has to go to the women whose sons are missing. This day will leave her no respite. She has not swallowed a thing, not even a few mouthfuls of water. As she is about to say goodbye, Eleke grips her hand: *Wait. Wait . . . I am not the only one hearing things since the fire.* She cannot say what messages others have received but she is sure that at least one of the women whose sons are missing is communing with her firstborn. *You will recognize her. Listen to your heart. She is a courageous woman. A worthy daughter of Emene. A valiant representative of Inyi. Do not bring her before the sages. She will walk in our name.*

Women are having their hair braided by servants in front of the compound's huts. Soon they will be wearing the cascading hairstyle that has become the latest fashion in the village. The style was created by one of the outcasts in the communal hut. Eyabe. The very person who the chief wants to see. The midwife feels a pang in her heart. Every one of the women whose sons are missing has a precise function in the village. Each brings something special to the community, has a unique sensibility.

As the names, faces and traits of these women come back to her, she reproaches herself for having forgotten this when she stood at a distance from the communal hut and coldly told them how they were going to live from then on. *I was not myself. I was not inside myself*, she murmurs. *Emene, our mother, pray help me, so that I do not err again. You, who are truth, justice and harmony, help me respect Your principles during the trials that beset our people. And*, she concludes choking back a sob, *forgive Your daughter for having acted without first asking for Your help.* Her eyes moist, she reaches the entrance to the compound. Daylight is waning. The sun, dressed in a woman's finery, turns into Enange, bathing the earth in a soft glow as it discreetly withdraws from human sight. Leaving room for the night. Then, it will set out on its subterranean journey to reappear after it has confronted and overcome the monster called Sipopo.

Ebeise is resolved to see the occupants of the communal hut before darkness falls. She cannot think any more. Too many emotions rioting inside her. Her only friend seemed so fragile, she fears she will never see her again. The words she wanted the midwife to hear, gathering for this purpose whatever little strength she had, drained her even more. Ebeise tries to think rationally. Humans do not decide who lives and who dies. Only Nyambe, the Uncreated, who is both Mother and Father of all that lives, knows the when and how. Right now, Ebeise, who others see as a forceful woman, feels only how weak she is. Sometimes she wishes she could be one of these women who do not attract attention, from whom nothing is expected. Her gait is too slow for her liking. The matriarch would like to run to Eyabe's home, reach the women in the communal hut as quickly as she can. Eyes fixed on the road ahead, she refuses to be distracted by anything happening around her. She does not smile at the sound of the men singing work songs as they rebuild a hut. She does not say a word to the two adolescents who are pounding the mbaa in rhythm. Yet all of them move her. So deeply she would go embrace each and every one if she were to listen to her heart. Immediately after the fire, decisions were made to eliminate all signs of the tragedy. No one spoke of it. No one knew what to say.

If Mwititi is also the shape that silences take, then it does not only hover over the communal hut. It is to dispel it that the men are singing and the girls are pounding the tubers to serve this evening. The fire, the disappearance of twelve males and the reclusion of ten women cast a shadow over everyday life. Surely she would not be one to claim otherwise. Ever since the great fire, sleep has abandoned her. Ever since, her co-wives sleep in the same hut. All day long, they do their best to avoid their children's questions when they ask what happened to their father. Did he leave them? They know him to be strong enough to confront any situation, so what could have happened?

Ebeise walks with her head bowed. Thus no one sees her tears, knows her distress. Crying helps her move forward more quickly. It does not rid her of the torment but it alleviates the anguish a bit. Her eyes are dry, her head high when she arrives at Eyabe's family's compound. She is greeted with deference. People step out of her way. The midwife seems to know exactly where to go, which surprises no one. Never have they seen this woman prey to hesitation. When she stands before Eyabe's hut, they all expect her to order Eyabe to come out and deliver the Council's sanction for daring to leave the communal hut. The midwife's voice is soft when she calls out, asks permission to enter. From outside, no one can see the occupant of the place, lying in a corner under the half wall that gives her some privacy. Everyone hears her reply: *Come in, our aunt.*

Ebeise steps inside. Her host does not take the trouble to get up but simply announces: *You will excuse me, our aunt. I am tired.* The old woman nods, sits on the ground, says nothing about the fact that Eyabe has cut her hair as mourners do. The cut locks are gathered in a clay pot to be burnt so that no one can use them for occult purposes. Without knowing why, the midwife does not inform Eyabe that the chief summoned her. Passing her hand over the face of the woman whose son is missing, she says: *You must not stay here.* The woman replies: *I was not planning to.* The midwife goes on: *Good. Let us burn your hair and leave this place.* Eyabe murmurs that she did not have the courage before, there were so many people around, there was this flower too, but she absolutely must dig up the placenta. She could not possibly leave without doing so. Again the old woman asks no questions. She has understood.

As soon as she crossed the threshold of this partly destroyed hut, a feeling of peace descended upon her. Not so much the removal of sadness as something else. Already, before being in Eyabe's presence, the matriarch knew she had to protect her, to shield her from the wrath of the Council. Now a certainty has taken hold of her: this woman is the one her friend spoke to her about. So, she explains to her: *There will be nothing there but earth now. You can take as much of it as you need—I will go with you. First, we will burn your hair.* As she whispers these words, the woman looks over the wall. Eyabe's co-wife is standing a few steps away trying to catch a word in passing. The midwife's glare makes her recoil and turn away. *This woman sent a child to the janea to denounce you*, Ebeise mutters. *We must go.*

*

Leaving Eyabe's compound, the two women ran into Ebusi who had just come out of the communal hut, she too covered in white clay. *Go find the janea*, the midwife instructed her. *Tell him that Eyabe cannot see him right now. Inform him that I will be spending the night in the communal hut and that I implore him to come to me there.* Before the slightest thought could take shape in the mind of Ebusi, who had plans of her own, the old woman led Eyabe away. Eyabe held in her hands the pot in which she had put a little earth, careful to preserve the flower discovered under the roots of the tree like a promise of rebirth. She did not see her co-wife Ekesi loitering around the hole where she had seen this unexpected flowering. You had to really cherish it, this small frail thing, to keep it intact. The rest of the family watched Ekesi, reminding her that it was not fitting to approach a tree under which a woman's placenta has been buried. It was, they explained, like touching the woman's private parts. Ekesi shrugged: *There is no tree there any more and no placenta either.* As she turned away, a thought firmly rooted in her heart. Later, when no one would suspect anything, she would drown the flower with her urine.

Seeing Eyabe come back with the midwife, the women whose sons went missing do not know what to think. They note their companion's shorn hair and imagine they will now be subjected to the ritual that will formally recognize their status as mourners. Some of the women shrink from the thought, preferring to be left with some hope. No matter how slight. Three weeks have not been enough for them to think of their sons as souls having to make their way to another world. They want to see them alive. If only they would appear with their brothers, a smile on their lips, and say: *It was silly. We lost our way in the bush.* If only the whole village would have a chance to laugh at these young initiates, still unable to find their way through the tangle of thick foliage around the clan's lands. If only the community would have a chance to organize a banquet and all gorge themselves for days on end to celebrate the return of the firstborns of this generation.

Other women do not care, do not dream of seeing their vanished sons again. For them it is high time to move on. Any change would be welcome. This seclusion, this exclusion cannot go on. Let their hair be shorn if that is what it takes to be permitted to have a normal life again. Let them be scarified if need be and have bark burnt to assist them in forgetting. This boy who is missing was always a thorn in their side. In spite of the passing years, they have never been able to see him without remembering the circumstances of his conception or the trials of his difficult birth, the looks to which they were subjected, all the rituals they had to perform. If their firstborn is dead, may his soul go where it pleases. Or may it be reincarnated wherever, but not through them. When the shadow came, they purposely turned away. Knowingly they made themselves deaf to its pleas. Yes, let their heads be shaven. Enough already. Like their sisters, they are hanging on the midwife's words.

Yet here she is now in front of them with no instructions and nothing to say about funerary rites or about the dance of the dead. Nothing to say to prepare them for the symbolic burial of those who are missing. She does not announce the making by the master-sculptor of statuettes materializing not the figure of the maloba but incantations and invocations. The sculptures are prayers. Those whose sons are missing need them. Alas, the midwife does not pronounce words of deliverance. All she does is exhort the residents of the communal hut to solidarity. The Council is seeking to lay blame for what happened. They will be the first to be found guilty. Ebeise does not tell them that in fact Eyabe is the only one in danger. The others could get away by submitting to rituals of purification. She keeps this from them in the hope of preserving unity.

The women whose sons are missing listen in silence. When the elder tells them she will stay in the communal dwelling with them from now on, it leaves them unperturbed. One of them murmurs: *Our aunt, would you like something hot? I will make it for you.* The elder replies: *Thank you my child. We will eat together. One of your sisters will help you.* For a moment, there is silence again. The women seem embarrassed to inhabit their own bodies. Ebeise has not lost her authority but she is addressing them with a benevolence that they have not known from her before. Never before has she allowed them to regard her as an equal. It would not be fitting. Familiarity is inconceivable between people who do not belong to the same generation. The women whose sons are missing wonder about the wisdom of letting a form of transgression be imposed upon them, be it by the clan's very well-respected midwife. Ebeise's competencies put her above the other women of the community. They make her an auxiliary of God who chose the female body to use as the forge in which to fashion humans. Camaraderie is not allowed. Instinctively, the outcasts bow their heads. One of them moves away from the group to join the woman who offered to cook.

Ebeise addresses those who remain in her company. *It will not be long,* she says, *before the shadow descends.* It would be good to light a fire around which they can gather. After sharing a meal, they will speak of the reasons that prompted the young master of mysteries to come question them at dawn. In the meantime, she will give them news of their family if they would like. As they busy themselves setting up a hearth in front of the communal hut, the midwife takes Eyabe aside. They move a few steps away. *I understand what you wish to accomplish. How will you go about it?* The woman looks at her intently: *I will be guided to the place. I have confidence.* The elder insists. The road could be long. It is not advisable to walk alone. And when does Eyabe intend to leave? She replies that she will walk in front of the day. The others will be asleep. Precisely at the time of the changing of the guard at the edge of the village. For a few moments, there will be no sentry. She will slip into the subtle interval separating night from day. The midwife nods as tears fill her eyes.

Making sure the others are not looking, Ebeise lays her right hand on the woman's forehead and whispers: *Emene, let your spirit descend upon your daughter. Intercede with Inyi on her behalf. Show her the way so she will return to us safe and sound.* Ebeise removes her amulet. She has never taken it off before. As she ties the pendant around Eyabe's neck, she explains: *I am an old woman now. This shield is of no use to me but it will protect you. Whoever seeks to hurt you will fall before touching you. Any weapon created or*

*thrown to destroy you will have no effect. May it be this
way, in the powerful name of Nyambe, creator of the sky,
the earth and the deepest depths.* After a moment of
silence, the midwife asks: *Would you like us to speak to
your sisters?—You will do so, Aunt Ebeise, once I have left
the village,* the woman replies. *Let the sun reach its
zenith. Then you will tell them.*

*

As they are about to join the other women, the janea
appears, followed by an escort of eight men. He is
wearing a musuka, with flaps that fall on either side
of his face, covering his neck and his upper shoulders, and a long sanja woven of plant fibre. This
clothing is worn exclusively by chiefs, as is the leopard skin draped over his shoulders. In his right hand,
Mukano holds a staff of command whose carved head
represents a leopard, reaffirming thereby the bonds
of his people with the king of the bush. Along the
whole length of the staff are the many painstakingly
engraved symbols tracing the history of his lineage.
Only a legitimate hand is authorized to touch this
rod. Planting it in the earth with each step he takes,
the chief walks in the presence of those who came
before him, under the protection of the forefathers,
in harmony with nature. His betambi leave the
imprint of his noble footsteps in the dust. A drum-
mer at his right solemnly announces his passage.

Ebusi, sent by the midwife to find the chief, is
walking some distance behind him. Because Mukano's

back is turned to her, she does not have to throw herself flat on the ground like the residents of the communal hut. She does not have to greet him with the customary praises and blessings. The chief and his retinue stop at a distance from the hut, so that she too is forced to stop. Her belly is crying out for food. She wishes she could sit down but it would be improper to make herself comfortable when Mukano is standing. The midwife kneels briefly in a show of respect, as the men do, and then steps forward, leaving behind the recluses lying flat on the ground. They cannot help but look up. It is the first time since they were gathered under this roof that Mukano has appeared in the vicinity. He seems concerned. It must be serious for him to come all the way here in person. Something has surely been kept from them. There is something suspicious about the midwife. The women whose sons have disappeared are tense. They know they should look down as propriety would have it, but they find it impossible to tear their eyes away from the scene. All the more since they hear nothing of what is being said.

Ebeise expresses her gratitude: *You who have been elevated, let me praise your greatness and thank you for having heard the call of a woman.* The two stand at a distance from the escort and from the occupants of the communal hut. Their exchange will remain a secret. Mukano nods: *I am obliged by your status in our community. Especially under these circumstances. I would have come sooner if I had not had to wait for my tracker's report. My brother has left the village. This does not bode well. I suppose you wanted to speak to me of something else.* In hushed tones, the midwife promptly relates her friend's words: *She insisted greatly. You know her. She never speaks lightly. Let it not be said that through you her words will fall to the ground.* Such a thought is far from his mind. Mukano shares old Eleke's opinion: it is time to appear before Njanjo, queen of the Bwele.

The words that have been reported to him contain, however, a very disturbing piece of information. The Bwele, it would seem, know what happened to the twelve missing men. Mukano thinks of his brother who, as the person in charge of trade, knows the neighbouring people better than anyone else. Is it time to prepare for war? Dismissing such thoughts, the chief turns his mind to diplomatic solutions. Since the clan's founding, the Mulongo have had no reason to fight their neighbours. The clan has warriors but they exist on principle. Their most trying combats are simply ceremonial jousting. The Mulongo warriors consider it an honour to have never spilt blood.

To drive away the foreboding that is beginning to tie his stomach up in knots, Mukano asks: *Why did you not bring Eyabe to me?* Crossing her arms behind her back, the matriarch steps back: *It is impossible for me to tell you anything more, janea, but our girl cannot appear before you for the moment. What do you mean?* he asks. *Is she indisposed?* The woman meets his gaze: *In a manner of speaking,* she says. *You will see her as soon as possible.* Then she adds: *Janea, do not rush off to the Bwele without consulting the ancestors, the maloba and*

Nyambe. I know you are anxious to get on your way . . . He nods, turns away and takes a few steps before turning back to her: *Woman, respect me as I respect you.*

The janea and his escort pass in front of Ebusi without seeing her. The beat of the drumming is softer now but just as grave. The woman waits until the procession has receded somewhat before moving. The sound of the armpit drum reaches her like a dirge. Daylight is gone. She has not done what she was planning to do. It breaks her heart. She is upset with herself that she did not have the courage to stand before the chief with kaolin on her face and shoulders. She is ashamed that she asked Eyabe's family for water to remove the white clay. Without looking her in the face, they brought her a calabash and, when she reached out for it, they put it on the ground. She washed her face in silence. Ebusi feels she has betrayed her son a second time, and this is unbearable. The cries she is holding inside strangle her as she slowly, step by step, joins the other outcasts of the clan.

*

Flames rise from the hearth. The women are now seated in a circle. They do not speak. From having thrown themselves on the ground to greet the chief, the front of their bodies is covered in earth. Some of them have earth on their cheeks, their lips, their chin. They avoid eye contact. The ordeal of being isolated from the clan united them only for a brief moment, at daybreak, when they had to hold on to one another to discover who was calling them outside the communal house. They have found no other reason since to surrender to one another. Eyabe did not join the circle. She sat by herself. It did not occur to her to prostrate herself before the chief. The white clay covering her face marks more than a physical distance from her companions. Even the women who do not wish to see their sons again did not go so far as to paint their faces and declare their sons dead. Ebusi, who started on the path of rebellion, lacked the boldness to bear the full weight of her acts. She sat down by the fire without a word.

Alone now where she stood talking to the chief, Ebeise observes the scene. The smells of the food reach her. She heads over to the group. She can feel the weariness of the women and recalls Eleke's clairvoyant words about the slackening spirit of sisterhood. Her knees creak as she sits down. Just as her broad rear end presses down on the ground, they hear a dull heavy sound. Eyabe has fallen over backwards. As she has not let go of the jar of earth gathered from under the tree, some of the silt has spilt out over her belly. Trembling from head to foot, she lets out a groan, her hands tightening around the recipient whose contents spill out again. At the same time, the women press their hands against their temples. They all open their mouths but only out of Ebusi's comes a cry so long and loud it races across the whole village, bouncing off the hillside where the nobles live, rebounding off the bark of trees, causing the stones to roll along the alleys separating the family compounds: *People, may you be my witness! Death already wants to take our sister! People* . . .

*

In the village compounds, everyone is frozen to the spot. Those with food in their mouths have trouble swallowing. Some spit out their food. The more intrepid try to swallow but the food gets caught in their throat, forms a ball that hardens, turns to stone. They all heard the scream from the communal hut. Does the shout herald more fire and losses? They should go see but the elders have ordered them not to approach this dwelling. They exchange silent looks. In their minds, the night of the fire takes hold. They remember another cry of distress, when the families were asleep. A woman, rushing out of her hut, yelled so powerfully that her voice must have reverberated throughout Creation, from the earth to the sky, from the sky to the depths: *People! People, may you be my witness!* First they thought it was a nightmare. They turned over on their mats to catch the sleep that was trying to slip away. Then they understood that a real living woman was wailing with heart-rending force.

Villagers came running, with sleep-blurry eyes. Flames flared from roof to roof at lightning speed. Other cries were heard, until a clamour of lament rose over the whole of Mulongo territory. They recall that the janea and his brother, who live up on the hilltop, could do nothing more than observe the disaster. They recall the rush to the bush when the fire threatened to consume the sanctuary with the collective reliquaries, the place where the bones, teeth and hair of the clan's ancestors are kept. The forefathers whose remains are preserved there are the greatest that the clan has brought into the world, the most honourable and worthy among them.

The night of the great fire, the women had gathered around the midwife. The spiritual guide had stayed to watch over the newly circumcised who still required his care. All the others had simply sought to save their skins. The community had begun to fall apart. At the first rays of dawn, the villagers had headed back to the village. They had stopped a few steps away, waiting for the whole clan to gather. No one wanted to go in alone. When all the groups scattered in the bush had returned, twelve men had been found missing: ten adolescents and two elders.

The villagers are reliving those fatal moments now. The memory is so strong that some regurgitate all the food they ate. The Mulongo understand that the fire is in them since the catastrophe. Many are unable to sleep. Many see themselves burn to death in their dreams and wake dazed and drenched in sweat. Many are thinking of the friend or brother they have not seen, about whom they do not speak. More than three weeks after the disappearance, the women have composed songs retelling the tragedy. For the time being, it is in low voices that they intone these laments of fury and loss. Walking by the communal hut to draw water, they do their utmost to avert their eyes from the women whose sons went missing. Nonetheless, something vibrates inside them.

From this vibration, the still-secret songs emanate that help them as they wait for the Council to lift the restrictions, so they can embrace a friend, a sister and say: *I too am weeping for our son.* The missing are not strangers. Especially for the women of the clan who watch over the children. Each woman entrusts her children to others when she is busy. Often, a son who is not well loved by the woman who gave birth to him will find a substitute mother in the community. The women who have been deprived by Nyangombe of the joys of childbearing grow attached to the offspring of another.

Each person is waiting for someone else to make a decision: to go to the communal hut or do nothing. Nothing, since they can clearly see there is no fire. Nothing, since any act driven by anxiety only gives body to weakness and could itself provoke the worst catastrophes. If anything serious is happening at the communal hut, there are ten women there, and they will know what to do, regardless of the riot of emotions in the depths of their hearts. In the privacy of their huts, when it will be time to rest, they will implore the invisible to protect them from whatever caused the cry.

The hands of the heads of the family do not tremble when they reach again into the communal dish. In silence, they expressed themselves. If the words of women must not fall to the ground, it is a matter of propriety to confine them to the privacy of the hut. Those who would like to talk will wait for the appropriate time. Meanwhile, the men will pretend not to notice that the women are not eating tonight. In two or three family compounds, the head of the family, before dipping his fingers into the dish, orders a son or a younger brother to go inform the Council. In two or three compounds only, because the initial response of the human heart to adversity is rarely to confront it. And then some of the dwellings are quite far from the communal hut. The woman's cry reaches these indistinctly. Some hear a sound that could be mistaken for the hooting of a night bird. These people do not even raise an eyebrow.

*

Mukano and his escort are at the foot of the hill. The ascent is being prepared to the sound of soft drumming. Just as the chief is about to plant his staff of authority in the ground, the cry of a woman is heard. A cry that contains all those that have not been released since the great fire. The janea freezes in midair. His men hold their breath. He does not speak. He tries to think. Quickly. Make up his mind. As chief, he ought to send someone to find out what happened, to wait for news. At the very least. For once, he does not feel like doing what he should. He is eager to go the Bwele, to learn what became of the men who are missing. He does not want to risk discovering anything this evening that could delay his departure.

He will spend the night in the sacred hut of the chiefdom without eating or drinking and will set out at daybreak.

Only his personal guard will go with him, not the warriors of the clan since they are not under his personal authority. When he suggested the search be pushed farther out into the bush and for a longer period of time, the Council members rose up like a single man to declare: *You will not send our offspring to face the unknown. What are you looking for in the end, Mukano? Do you want our boys to be swallowed up by something we cannot even name?* Their procrastinating has made him lose too much time already. Mukano looks up, turns in the direction of the cry. The communal hut is out of sight. But distance alone, he thinks, would not prevent him from seeing flames rise if it were on fire. During the great fire, the sky glowed from afar. There is nothing of the sort now. Everything seems to be more or less in order, even if this cry manifests a disturbance.

The man tells himself that the midwife will do what needs to be done, she will ask for help from her son if need be. He can leave it to Ebeise to deal with the unfamiliar turn of events that has caused one of the outcasts to disrupt the clan's tranquillity. Without realizing it, the janea murmurs: *There is no fire. Women cry without rhyme or reason.* One of his escorts hears him and chuckles. There is no word in the Mulongo language to describe the icy look the chief casts at him. Mukano plants his staff of command in the earth, leans on it so that those whose memory is engraved in its wood will support him. He has waited all too long. When he reaches the hilltop, he asks for presents to be prepared for queen Njanjo. Then he commands them: *Let no one disturb me under any circumstance. We will leave at dawn.*

*

The matriarch instructs Ebusi to be silent. The elder approaches Eyabe̲ with self-assurance, pins her to the ground. She must wait, listen. A force is here that demands to be expressed. Anyone who covers her face in white clay communicates with the other world. The women sitting near the communal hut rise. Some join the midwife. Others step back, dust the dirt off their bodies, thinking they will be spared nothing today. They gaze vacantly into the distance.

Ebeise̲ says: *Death will not take her.* Soon the woman's body calms down, slackens. Eyabe̲'s flesh becomes like clay into which the midwife's hands sink. Drops of sweat bead on her forehead. She shakes her head from side to side, lets out a moan. The midwife releases her for a moment, grabs the jar of earth gathered under the tree, gently sets it on the ground. These words escape Eyabe̲'s lips: *Mother, there is nothing but water. The way back is gone. There is nothing any more but water.*

The rest is inaudible, but these words revive the memory of the nine other women of the shadow that came to them, prompting them to stretch their necks to see, though they saw nothing. Yet all keep silent.

When the elder asks that they help her carry Eyabe into the communal hut, they know the night will be long. Three of them join the midwife in carrying the body of their companion. The others rekindle the fire around which they gather to keep watch. The fire will hold darkness at bay.

The Shadow Speaks

Mutango is busy. He knows the Council is meeting. His attendance is required at such an assembly. He will find an excuse. If need be, he will plead indigestion, which will surprise no one, even though four members of the Council know he is in excellent health. He received them at the crack of dawn after he left the communal hut of the women whose sons are missing. The man hastened to inform them about the shadow seen hovering over the women's dwelling. Without waiting to hear what they thought, he shared his feelings with them, adding, perfidiously, that the current rulership had not taken the measure of the danger. Sacrifices should have been performed the day after the fire. The circumstances called for the slaughter of animals.

The shrubs around him risk piercing his paunch with their thorns. The dignitary has lost the habit of venturing out alone in the bush. He has not stepped foot there without an escort since his initiation, or at least not this far. When he has secret commerce with the invisible, he goes to a peaceful clearing he found no more than a quarter-day's walk from the village, even a little less, there and back. This time, the situation compels him to travel a long distance without escort. His belly hangs over the belt of his manjua, revealing the abdominal scarifications that form dark keloids around his navel. His necklaces, bracelets and amulets will not protect him from the prick of thorns and the fierce itching caused by the masibo whose leaves rub hard against his calves. To top it off, he forgot to bring his machete. One of his servants always takes charge of this. His cutlass with a curved blade is perfect for killing but of little help here.

The man advances, obstinate, braving the assaults of nature. The hostility of the environment keeps him alert, which is not such a bad thing. When a branch gets caught in the tips of his braids decorated with nervures and grains, he suppresses a profanity, wrestles with the brazen thing, regains his freedom at the cost of a little sweat, continues on his way. The soles of his huge feet spread out, crush the muko̲ iy̲o insensitive to everything that covers the ground or is hidden in it. To know the man's temperament, this is where one should look—or deep into his eyes. Mutango does not pamper his feet as he does the rest of his opulent envelope. They are dry, rough, made for trampling all that exists. Feet without fear, without pity.

To make his journey more pleasant, the dignitary has brought along a pouch filled with pieces of smoked meat that he devours as he walks. He has forgotten to bring a goatskin bottle that he would have filled with a tangy juice made from bongo̲ngi leaves.

As a result, the meat, which he does not bother to chew properly, overflows his oesophagus. The dignitary puts to use his powerful salivary glands, produces the amount of liquid needed for his organism to assimilate the meat. He burps profusely, cleans his teeth with a splint of bobimbi whose bark is known for its disinfecting properties. The frequent use of this plant is what gives his smile its dazzling whiteness. His is a smile that is never an expression of joy. Instead of lighting up when he smiles, his eyes turn red, then dark. The only thing that prevents others from turning on their heels and running when they see this is the respect they owe to his rank. He enjoys this. The capacity to terrify others galvanizes him to the point of laughter at times. The fat dignitary will then grunt like a warthog, which only intensifies the characteristics he shares with this animal. All he is missing are the tusks. But appearances can be deceptive: he carries them in his head.

He does not have far to go. From time to time, he stops to catch his breath, turns to make sure nothing is moving behind him in the shrubs, that his brother did not have him followed. Nothing stirs but the wind, in reality not even the wind since it can barely penetrate the thick foliage around him. The man continues on his way. Soon his steps take him to a boulder. He carefully planned his route to avoid inhabited areas. Bekombo, the great Bwele city, lies a half-day's journey from this boulder. Mutango knows the Bwele better than anyone else in his community. As the agent responsible for trade, he is the one who comes most regularly to meet them, exchange food and goods for products that his people do not produce or only in small quantities. The Bwele are more prosperous than the Mulongo, more powerful too. Their territory covers a huge area peopled by the many clans they have subdued over the ages.

At the boulder, Mutango turns left. This changes nothing for his merciless feet even though he is now travelling on a nearly smooth path cleared through the heart of the bush by hunters from the surrounding area. At the end, a stream flows peacefully in the shade of giant trees. White flowers with delicate petals and yellow pistils shooting up to the sky emit an odour of rotting flesh. The dignitary stops, not to draw water to facilitate his digestion but because he has a meeting here. He looks for a dry place to rest his imposing posterior that weighs on his legs. With his right foot, in a single thrust, he sweeps aside a pile of leaves, revealing the ochre earth underneath. Just as he is about to sit down, he hears a reedy voice: *You are late, son of Mulongo. The sun has moved three times since I am here waiting for you.*

The person who just spoke is so short he could be mistaken for a child if his cheeks and chin were not covered with a thick beard. He is dressed in hunting clothes made of furry animal skin. This disgusts Mutango, who sees it as a lack of refinement. The Mulongo treat skins before wearing them, all the more so since animal hides retain heat which is unnecessary at this time of year. He says nothing. The short man—a hunter so formidable that no one in his community would think of jeering at his size—is not sweating. Mutango sets his rear end down on the ground as he was about to do before he was interrupted, lets out a powerful sigh. He looks up at the face of the complainer and greets him: *Son of Bwele, how did you leave the night?* The man dismisses the question with an impatient wave of the hand: *Night departed long ago and I left it as I entered it.*—*Well, well,* replies Mutango, *let us talk about our business. What have you to tell me?*—*Not so soon, Son of Mulongo,* says the hunter. *You owe me.*

Mutango understands he will have to pay before being served. This does not coincide with his view of the world. He must make sure that the merchandise is worth it. In fact, the Mulongo dignitary is not running much of a risk. What he has brought in payment is not exactly what his interlocutor expects but it is important not to give in too quickly. The two of them will have other arrangements to make in the near future, or at least he thinks they will. These negotiations will sway things in his favour. If he gives in to paying before evaluating the merchandise, he will lose the authority and credibility he needs for future transactions. The notable reaches into the pouch containing his ration of meat for the trip, pulls out a cutlass with a curved blade, of the type that only the master blacksmiths of his people know how to make. The handle is delicately carved, the sharp metal blade glistens, reflecting the rare rays darting through the dense leafage of the tall trees. He sets the weapon down by his side with surprising delicacy considering the size of his hands, and turns to the hunter: *What you asked for is here. I would not dare deceive you when we are alone here. After all, you wield a weapon better than I do . . . Now tell me.*

His eyes glued to the wrought-wood handle, the hunter nods slowly, delivers the expected information. A column of men travelled across the bush for days, carefully avoiding the villages. But they did not erase the traces of their passage. Being an excellent tracker, he succeeded in following their trail, to some extent. These men reached Bwele country—a brisk day's walk from where they are right now—and went on. They could not have gone farther than the coast. Beyond, there is no territory where humans can travel. *Are you telling me*, Mutango asks, *that if I go to what you call the coast, I can find out who these men were and what became of them?* The hunter replies forthrightly: *I conducted this investigation for your sake even though you did not ask me to. It was not very hard to do.*

The hunter takes a step forward, crouches opposite him, teeth clenched, looking him straight in the eye. Their faces would touch if it were not for the difference in height that gives the notable a slight advantage. The silence between them becomes a compact substance. Mutango has obtained the information he initially requested. Additional details will require more than a cutlass, be it as beautiful and dangerous as this one. He is not in a hurry. If he has not yet reached down to give the object to the hunter before getting up and turning on his heels, it is because he is thinking. The next step will be for him to go personally to the coast, see with his own eyes if the missing men are there. Whatever the hunter might say now, he will have to make this trip. He clasps the cutlass, hands it to the hunter: *Use it well.* The small man holds the knife, glides his finger over the blade. In a low voice he asks: *Has your Minister of Rites performed the necessary ceremony?*

Mutango does not intend to tell him that his clan no longer has a mediator between this world and the others, only a sorcerer's apprentice whose face betrays the great bewilderment that has bedevilled him since his father went missing. He confines himself to an indirect reply: *No need for concern. A tool such as this is governed by the spirit of its owner. Tell me about those who live at the edge of Creation.* The hunter shrugs. His people know the coastlanders well. They are neighbours. The people who live on the brink of the world are terribly pretentious, to his mind. Ever since they met the foreigners who came across the waters, they see themselves as equals of the gods. Their new friends provide them with fabric unknown in this part of misipo. They also give them weapons, jewellery and things for which we have no names. Finally, the coastal residents, who describe themselves as children of the water even though everyone knows they were driven to the extremity of the land in the course of old battles for territory, now claim to be brothers of the men with hen feet. Mutango looks at him wide-eyed. *Men with hen feet?* he asks excitedly. The hunter realizes he has said too much, refuses to go on.

As the hunter is about to stand up, Mutango takes hold of his arm. He needs to know more. *Listen, I am not asking you anything about the procession of men. I am satisfied. But I would like you to explain what you mean by men with hen feet.* The Bwele man shrugs again. The last time he was on the coast, where he sometimes goes to sell his game, he saw these creatures. *These people cover themselves from head to toe*, he says. *What they wear on their legs makes them look like hens, which is why the locals gave them the name 'men with hen feet'. The notables do not speak of them with so little respect. They call them 'foreigners who have come across the waters from pongo'. To tell you the truth, I have never approached them.*

Shooting a glance at the sky, Mutango sees that time has gone by. His questions about the men with hen feet have got the hunter talking. Fascinated by these creatures with whom he has never conversed, the man tells him all he knows and what is said about them. They have never come to Bwele country but, because they are neighbours to the Coastlanders, he has learnt some surprising things. It is said that the foreigners are emissaries of distant dignitaries seeking alliances with their counterparts on this side of Creation. To demonstrate their goodwill, they have showered gifts on the coastal princes, which is why the latter have been calling them their brothers and are lodging them on their land.

It has been some time that their vessel is anchored off the coast, a huge pirogue covered in material intended to imprison the wind. The Coastlanders have given them women to keep them company, servants to make sure the guest huts in which they are housed are comfortable. The hunter, whose name Mutango has learnt is Bwemba, suddenly lowers his voice to share the most astonishing revelations. The men with hen feet are said to have weapons that spit fire and kill from a distance. They thus avoid hand-to-hand combat. Mutango is already thirsting to have one of these devices. During this exchange of confidences, the two men told each other their names. They had tacitly avoided doing so until now, out of prudence. To reveal your name is to entrust the other with a precious part of yourself, to lay yourself bare. All you have to do is whisper someone's name during a ritual to attack them from afar, expose them to evil spirits. So until now they only addressed each other by referring to the founders of their respective peoples. One was called Son of Bwele, the other Son of Mulongo.

An idea has just occurred to Mutango. Bwele country is a day's walk from where they are meeting. The hunter will be spending the night somewhere in the bush, probably in a shelter midway to his home. If they leave together now, they will arrive before nightfall. The notable will not have to explain himself to the men that his brother has entrusted with the task of keeping watch on the outskirts of the village, from dusk to dawn. This is how it has been since the fire. Also, Mutango absolutely wants to discover more about the men with hen feet. He does not know why but something tells him there is a connection between these foreigners with their huge vessel and those who have gone missing. No beast from the bush, no matter how fierce, could have gobbled up ten new initiates and two adults. He may be mistaken, but if he is not, he will know before his brother does.

So he addresses Bwemba in these terms: *Soon daylight will fade. It is time for you to start on your way. Let me accompany you, if you will.* The Bwele hunter looks at him wide-eyed. *Yes,* the dignitary confirms. Bwemba asks him how he will explain his presence in Bwele country when he has not come to trade. *Have no fear. I will go present myself to Queen Njanjo. Let us be on our way. We will reach our destination at noon, which is good, because there will be a lot of activity and no one will notice us.* Mutango does not know yet how he will proceed. He wants to go to the coast, see with his own eyes what his companion has described. The problem is he did not prepare himself for such a long trip. Of course, he took his passport with him, a small earthenware mask that he always wears. It is hanging from one of his many necklaces. It says where he comes from, his age group, his responsibilities and his status in Mulongo society.

But he has not brought gifts to offer the noblemen of the coast. Nothing of worth that would serve not so much as a medium of exchange for merchandise but as testimony of respect. Admittedly, it would not be appropriate to appear before Queen Njanjo without placing something of value at her feet, but he is sure he will find a way to be forgiven, an excuse for his negligence. On the other hand, the coastal princes do not know him. They will have no reason to welcome him favourably. He cannot possibly meet them during this first visit to their territory. Never mind. The man is ready to hug the walls when he is in coastal country if that is what it takes to see the foreigners and know the real reasons for their presence on this side of Creation. If they have come across the waters from pongo, they undertook a long perilous journey. It is hardly likely that people would put themselves through such trials simply to make new friends.

As Mutango sees it, communities have interests, not feelings. If the leaders of the men with hen feet sent their emissaries over such a great distance, they must want something. And they want it for themselves, not for the people of the coastal country. He will find out the truth, will see with his own eyes the strange attire that makes people look like fowl. If possible, he will inspect this vessel that they say is gigantic. His own people have only the most trivial relationship with water—they drink it, use it for washing up, for cleaning. And now here he is setting out to discover how it is possible to use it as a passageway between two territories. The Coastlanders' pirogues, as described by Bwemba, already seem to be the most extraordinary devices. Deep down, the Mulongo notable even has doubts about the humanity of the men with hen feet. But ultimately, anyone can distinguish between a man and a spirit. If his companion claims that the strangers are human, he might as well believe him. For the time being.

Mutango does not share his thoughts with the hunter. They walk without a word, alert to the sounds of nature around them. There is not a living soul on the paths they take. Not an animal, not even a rodent scurrying through the shrubs, causing the tiny leaves of the sensitive muko iyo to recoil, close as a defence against aggressions. This is of no concern to Mutango, busy as he is mentally preparing what he will say to the Bwele, then to his own people when he returns to his community. Indigestion will not be a good enough excuse to explain an absence of several days. Most likely they will imagine he succumbed to the same fate as the missing men. He is thinking of using this to his advantage, inventing for the occasion one of the stories infused with mysticism that he is so good at telling, as long as no one asks him too many questions. Dusk is nearing when the two reach the hunting shelter where Bwemba was planning to spend the night alone.

The hut is made of branches to blend into the environment. It would be easy to miss, so small is this shelter built to house a short man. The notable could not possibly fit inside. He will sleep on the ground by the makeshift shelter. He has enough meat in his bag to last until the next day. No need for concern in that regard. As for any animals that may prowl the bush, he knows them all, has nothing to fear from them. In fact, the reason Mutango is such a poor hunter is that he feels more affinity with the animal kingdom than with the human species. When he devours large quantities of animal meat, it is always with love. The ingested meat makes him one with the animal, which is why he takes particular care in choosing the meat he eats. He has been chewing on pieces of smoked monkey since he left the village. The monkey is agile and cunning. The cunningness is what interests him. He leaves the meat of goats and poultry to commoners, preferring by far grilled warthog, a not-very-well-liked animal, incapable of affection and hard to capture.

The members of his clan are not allowed to eat leopard for it is the guardian of his people and the lord of the bush. When they first settled on their present land, the Mulongo ancestors had to offer up humans to him in sacrifice, in order to live in peace on their new territory. Mutango granted himself permission to transgress this rule on several occasions, not only to discover the taste of leopard meat but also, and especially, to acquire the animal's power. To think like a leopard. To be as capable of cruelty. To get to know solitude, to be content with it. To be attached to no one. It had not been so easy for him to get a hold of the meat of the sacred animal. Mutango, then almost twenty, enticed his clan's best hunter by promising him the hymen of one of the daughters of the chief, that is, his and Mukano's father. His clan does not attach importance to the virginity of women. After a theoretical initiation to pleasure, girls are invited to put into practice the teachings they receive from their elders, preferably before marriage. It is unthinkable that a woman, when she is given to a man, would not know what to do in their intimacy. But he who was to become the young Mutango's right-hand man had a fixation on the tight vagina of virgins and so he came almost completely undone when he was assured that he would be the first to possess the body of a princess.

Ready to take all manner of risk, he delivered, still warm, the dead body of the lord of the bush. Mutango thanked him, extended a goatskin filled with mao to him, watched him collapse under the effect of the sedative in the drink. He plunged the curved blade of his cutlass into the hunter's chest, pulled out the still-beating heart, tore off a piece with his bare teeth, let the blood pour into a calabash, drank it down, holding his breath, his head buzzing with a litany of incantations. Then, the still-young man that he was, took the time to dismember the leopard, to cut off the meat with which he secretly nourished himself, absorbing nothing else for several days. As a souvenir of this great moment, he keeps the canines of the animal in a talisman of his own making. Buried under layers of dikube bark, they are contained in a flat square-shaped amulet that he displays on his broad chest.

Gorged on forbidden meat, the murderer mourned his victim. Like the rest of the community, he attended the funeral, moaned when the elders planted a tree trunk to symbolize the corpse that was nowhere to be found. Then Mutango waited for the invisible to start working for him, to set him up on the stool of authority. He is waiting still. He has even begun to think that someone in his brother's maternal family must have had recourse to occult powers. There is no other explanation for his failure. Mukano has been chief all this time because someone spilt blood for him. Someone has dirtied his hands for him. The hypocrite comes to Mutango's home, insults him for lying with one of his daughters, but he is no better. Anyway, if Nyambe deemed a father's desire for his offspring reprehensible, he would not allow a man's penis to stiffen when a child born of his loins walks by. Everything that exists is the work of the divine. Good and Evil are contingent. Good is what pleases, what profits. Evil is all the rest.

Dreaming of the day when he will hold the staff of command—and not only the staff given to him as an emissary when he goes to trade with the Bwele—Mutango plans to put an end to the sentimentalism that his brother presents as a matter of morality. It will be a new era, as brutal as reality. Power will be passed down from father to son. If the chief has two offspring of the same age, they will be put to the test. The one who will have demonstrated a greater lack of emotion and an ability to impose his views will be appointed chief. The end will justify the means. After making sure that the warriors are even better trained, he will send them to explore areas that are off limits today. Everyone knows the earth is not made up of Coastlanders, Bwele and Mulongo alone. They all know it because the history of the Mulongo migration is still told to young initiates. He will set out to see. Conquer new lands. Expand the power of his people. Rival the Bwele. Dominate them one day, why not? As this thought comes to him, the man directs a piercing glance at his companion.

In front of the shelter, Bwemba seems to be asking himself how the two can spend the night there. Mutongo reassures him: *Do not worry, son of Bwele, I will sleep under the stars.* The hunter does not insist, disappears into the hut. Mutango inspects the surroundings, finds a tree with long branches nearby. It is not rainy season but he would rather take cover. He lies down on the rough ground using his bag as a headrest, closes his eyes, wonders for a moment about the number of such shelters scattered across the bush. The Mulongo have one, only one; he uses it on his trips to the Bwele. Since there are many more Bwele, they may very well have several retreats like this.

The dignitary dismisses these futile thoughts but does not fall asleep straight away. He wonders what was said this morning in the Council meeting. Surely his brother sent for him. He can no longer bribe the guards at the entrance to the village, persuade the Council to believe that he never left the village. He needs an excuse, he will find one.

*

Daylight has fled. The dusk is as deep as the darkest hour of the night. Not a ray of light filters through the branches of the trees whose foliage bends with the wind. Mutango cannot sleep. From inside the hut, Bwemba's snoring reaches him, like a hooting uttered to challenge eternity. How can such a small body produce such a huge hullabaloo and with such regularity? It is a mystery to him. He tries to focus his thoughts on a precise point, to no avail. An uncommon anxiety takes hold of him, he whose heart is usually moved by nothing. He feels himself invaded by a presence whose thickness envelopes him, pins him to the ground.

Mutango struggles, calls out to his companion. The hunter, no doubt deafened by his own snoring, hears nothing. Mutango gets a grip on himself, tries to determine the exact nature of what is attacking him. The memory comes back to him of the shadow that hovered over the hut where the women whose sons were missing were staying. He had given an explanation of the phenomenon to those members of the Council who had gathered at his place, but it was without really understanding it. Nailed to the ground, his intuition tells him that the shadow at daybreak and the force that is keeping him from moving are connected. Since it is impossible for him to move, he concentrates to allow his spirit, which cannot be held captive, to escape and observe. The spirit's eye sees and hears all. The proximity of such trees as the bobinga and bongongi, known for their mystical virtues, are of precious help. Mutango will know what to make of it. He will not shy away from a fight, if that is what this is. Then he will return to his body.

The notable keeps quiet so that his adversary will not guess his intentions. Leaving his body could take time. The risks are great if his assailant perceives his strategy. Inwardly, the man recites the words that allow the spirit to detach itself from the body. He has only just begun the litany when a voice speaks to him. Only he hears the voice, and not only because Bwemba is sleeping soundly. It is a consciousness that is speaking to his. As this voice penetrates him, Mutango realizes it is carried by a choir. It all happens very quickly: *Uncle,* the voice asks, *why are you walking with that one? Do you not know that the Bwele cast their nets over us?*

When Mutango opens his eyes, darkness shrouds the bush. The anxiety is gone. He is no longer pinned to the ground. He heard these words distinctly, with all the distress and anger they contained. Trusting in no one, certainly not in Bwemba, he calls on the invisible not to let sleep take him. His fellow traveller is hiding something from him, of this Mutango is convinced. He thought he could deceive Bwemba by offering him a cutlass over which the Mulongo Minister of Rites had performed no rite, but it seems that the Bwele hunter was playing him, and much more seriously. He needs this man to go with him into Bwele territory. The crucial thing is to stay alert in case Bwemba is planning to murder him.

Mutango sits up. He cannot stay there lying on the ground lest sleep overpower him. It is a long time before the break of day when they will set out again. Night has fallen completely, so it is too late to think about setting out on his own. He leans against the tree that was supposed to protect him in his sleep and listens. Maybe the voice will speak again. He waits. It was a furtive, uncanny voice; it seemed to emanate from a multitude. The notable keeps his imagination from drifting, but something inside him is on edge. He knows this voice. Each of the voices that together called him uncle. Spirits would have no reason to speak to him like this. The memory of the shadow hovering over the communal hut takes hold of him again.

He fixes his eyes upon his surroundings, trying to distinguish the shadows from one another: those that belong to the night and the others. It is impossible. The darkness is too dense. Mutango decides against kindling a fire for fear he awaken the hunter who might grow suspicious seeing that he is not asleep. His sense of sight will be of no help to him. He must listen and feel. To enhance his concentration, he closes his eyes, relaxes his muscles. As his body goes limp and his breathing slows and steadies, his faculties are heightened. He becomes pervious to everything, at one with the faintest element present in the bush.

Mutango hears what usually escapes human hearing: a column of ants conversing, beetles laying eggs, tiny clumps of grass growing. He senses. Not only the breeze hiccoughing through the thicket or the earth creeping very slowly under his buttocks and his thighs that are resting flat on the ground. There is also the shadow, a shadow that is not the night quivering in the heart of the dark night. It is icy. Everything is alive in this place. Everything, except this shadow. It holds a multitude and they now belong to another dimension. Mutango listens attentively to the story they tell, discovering that it is not destined to him alone. At this very moment, it is possible that others are hearing the tale. The man gives his full attention to those who now describe themselves as prisoners of the land of water.

*

By midday, they have still not reached the gates of Bekombo, the great Bwele city. Mutango is by no means as light-footed as his companion who must slow his pace for him. The sky has already taken on the purplish hue that announces the entry of the sun into the subterranean world when the two men presented themselves to the guards posted at the edge of the city. The verifications do not take long. One of them is from there and is well known. The other comes to these parts often and has been seen before. The guards cast a distracted glance at his passport mask. The two men move on while the guards return to their bawdy talk.

Bwemba suggests that the son of Mulongo let the queen's entourage know he is there. He may not be able to pay his respects this evening, but high-ranking foreigners must make their presence known to the court. As he starts down the main street of the town, Mutango cannot stop admiring the architecture of the buildings whose walls and roofs are decorated with delicately painted friezes. He studies the doors made of epindepinde, a dark wood that is not used in his village because his people associate it with shadowy powers. Unquestionably, he thinks, the forces of darkness must have virtues if a material that symbolizes them proves to be of such elegance.

He also looks at the clothes of the few people lingering about, noting the fine Bwele craftsmanship that works wonders with looms for weaving esoko. Among his people, even the most delicate textiles are made by beating fabric, a technique that does not call for the same degree of virtuosity. Mutango suddenly feels rather backward and a little ragged. His companion's hunting clothes made him forget the textile artistry of the Bwele. He is comforted somewhat by the fact that the Mulongo are more adept at working hide. The chiefs of his community have ceremonial garments in leopard that testify to their skill. The costume is so beautiful that it imparts poise and authority to the wearer. Even when the individual is as insignificant a person as his brother Mukano. One day, Mutango is convinced, he will wear the mpondo and hold the staff of command. He feels close, so very close to his goal. A voice resonates in him, affirming that this unexpected incursion into Bwele country is a turning point, one of those moments that allows destiny to be accomplished. Thinking of this, Mutango puffs out his fat chest, as if to receive the honours owed to his greatness.

Yes, soon he will be chief of the Mulongo. His chest will be marked by ritual scarifications; etched directly into his flesh will be the immaterial bond that unites all of the clan's chiefs with those who came before them, reminding them daily that their existence belongs to the community. The begotten carry within the living and the dead. Does not the Mulongo motto say: *I am because we are?* At the sight of a weaver putting his material away, the dignitary stops, observes the instrument used to make fabric in esoko. Suddenly, he turns to Bwemba, struck, even outraged by what he sees: *Men do this work?* Bwemba nods: *The craft used to be passed down to the male members of a single family line. Now, it is a simple trade learnt from a master. This man is putting his things in order because night is coming. It is forbidden to weave after sunset.* Although Mulongo cannot readily distinguish the different parts of the loom, he tries to assess the difficulty of an activity he thinks should be a woman's chore. Men have better things to do. Seeing the craftsman hurry around his workbench, step through the doorway to his home on the side, the Mulongo notable thinks about the future when he will rule over this people, restore the natural prerogatives of men.

They arrive at the royal compound after an excessively long walk for Mutango, who can barely feel his legs after the journey through the bush. In a bustle of activity, preparations are underway for an audience with the queen—an uncommon event at this time of the day. Such a reception is usually not held this late. But they are already busy with arrangements because Her Majesty will sit on her stool of authority at the crack of dawn. Bwele dignitaries, recognizable from

their clothing, headdress, adornments and scarifications, have been summoned. Orders are being issued
to distraught servants who have little experience with
such special audiences. The royal estate is a circular
area inside a clay enclosure. Eight dome-shaped
constructions hug the curve of the surrounding
wall. Four of these are big. They house the queen's
family and her closest advisors. Three other smaller
buildings are reserved for servants. The last one
houses high-ranking visitors. This is where Mutango
should be spending the night.

The queen's house stands out as it is slightly
greater in circumference and height than the homes
of the nobility. The tumult is at its peak at the centre
of the courtyard, in front of the open doors of houses
that seem to be keeping watch over each other. Servants are lining up caryatid stools for the eminent
members of the audience, unrolling between the two
rows a fabric in esoko which has the unique feature
of being specially embroidered by the Bwele women.
The Mulongo notable is surprised to see them spread
a fabric directly on the ground. The hunter tells him
the textile is not made to be worn. The material,
woven by men as always, is considered both a piece
of furniture and a decorative object. Once the weavers
have completed their work, it is entrusted to a
specific category of women—he does not specify
which—to be embroidered with designs of their
devising.

This makes no sense to Mutango. Where he
comes from the craftspeople are attached, of course,

to the beauty of their work but beauty is determined by the correspondence between the object and its profound meaning. And meaning is precisely what eludes him here. Without questioning the hunter any further, sensing that he is not telling him everything, he continues to examine this fabric made to walk on, as if the earth was not good enough, as if it was not absolutely primordial to maintain strong bonds with it. When the hunter adds that the material in question is also used to wrap the bodies of noblemen before burial, the fat dignitary stops trying to understand. The same material cannot be dedicated to such different uses. It is absurd. Apparently no one has taken an interest in the newcomers. The notable asks his companion: *What exactly is going on?*

Just then one of the Bwele noblemen cries out: *Bring him over here! It is out of the question that he appear before Njanjo in that state.* Then, turning to a woman of his caste, he adds: *We are in complete agreement— his face, torso and upper limbs must be painted. Otherwise our sovereign's authority will be diminished.* Someone suggests that such a measure seems unreasonable. The Coastlanders receive these individuals as they are and deal with them on an equal footing. *You speak of equality*, retorts the man whose proposal has been challenged. *I maintain that our coastal brothers are not indifferent to the appearance of these foreigners from pongo. If we are to judge from their complexion, they must be spirits, no doubt revenants, and not ours.*

It is inconceivable to let the queen appear in front of this person. The mere fact that he came without announcing his arrival shows he thinks it is permissible to do whatever he likes. The Coast-landers, who are providing him with accommodations, should have sent an emissary to inform the Bwele, to let them know of their guest's ridiculous desire to come and go as he pleases. *They gave him an escort of four men whose fate will be decided later. What matters right now is the fact that they did not trouble themselves to establish a passport for him in due form. Thus, we know nothing about this person. Nothing at all. And since it is better to be safe than sorry, I say the individual should appear in restraints before Her Majesty. We will have his teeth cleaned, since he does not seem to be familiar with this practice. And a colouring should be applied to give him a human aspect.* Njanjo must remain master of herself to make the decisions that will engage the Bwele people as a whole. *Bring him over here,* the dignitary repeats. *And bring the dye too. It will be safer to cover him from head to toe.*

Suddenly, a woman's voice is heard. The hunter and his Mulongo companion did not notice her watching them. Yet she was right there from the start, standing with her back against one of the great pillars at the entrance to the compound, at somewhat removed from the agitation. *Watch out,* she warns, staring in their direction. *We cannot accomplish this act in the presence of just anybody. There is an intruder here.* A silence as heavy as a buma trunk descends upon everyone. All eyes converge on Bwemba and Mutango. The hunter kneels in a sign of respect before the woman who has just spoken. He bends over until his forehead touches the dust, holds the position for a long time. Mutango is dumbfounded by this mark of submission on the part of a man to a woman. Without straightening up, Bwemba tugs vigorously on the notable's manjua, forcing him to lower himself too. Mutango consents to putting one knee on the ground, then the other. But something deep inside keeps him from prostrating himself. The hunter's raspy voice comes to him as in a dream: *Hail, Princess Njole. Please forgive the intrusion of this man. I wanted to introduce him to the court as is required by law. He is the Mulongo trade emissary. I did not know . . .*

The princess cuts him off: *You could not have known. Exceptionally, you will have to accommodate our guest under your roof. He will appear in court tomorrow at which time we will demonstrate our deference to him.* Bwemba nods in agreement. Still on his knees, he edges back before allowing himself to get up. Mutango, on the other hand, has not moved an inch. Even if he wanted to, he could not follow suit. Moving back while still on his knees requires a mental preparation that he lacks; but that is not his only problem—the fat notable does not feel physically equipped to imitate the hunter without making a laughing stock of himself. He is not even sure he will be able to get back onto his feet without losing his balance. So Mutango stays there motionless under Princess Njole's mischievous gaze. After a while, the woman claps her hands, waves two servants over: *Kindly help our neighbour get up. Bwemba, you will leave him in the care of your people who will make sure he is comfortable. I will be expecting you at the break of day. Alone.*

*

It is the first time that Mutango has been invited into a Bwele home. His meetings with Bwemba were confined to discussions on Bekombo's trade square on market days. If he had not spoken up, asked his companion for a favour, things would not have gone much farther. This evening he sees a reality that he had suspected at times without really giving it much thought. The small hunter is a respected man in his community. His compound, enclosed in manner of all those belonging to people of elevated social status, comprises three standard-size houses and one small one for servants. The latter throw themselves at his feet when they see him. With a nonchalant wave of the hand, he invites them to get up, gives them instructions. Mutango takes pleasure in seeing the humble attitude of the hunter's wives in their husband's presence. Bwemba's two wives come out of their separate dwellings to meet them. They do not go so far as to kneel before the men but they greet them graciously: *Welcome back to your home, our husband. And welcome, also, to you stranger.*

While Bwemba explains who his guest is, the reason why he has to spend the night, Mutango shamelessly studies the women, feels their flesh with his eyes, weighs their breasts, rejoices that there is at least one area where they can only submit. The torches attached to the front of the dwellings illuminate the courtyard well enough for the Mulongo notable to get a good eyeful. His host's voice pulls him out of his thoughts: *I leave you in their hands. I will see you tomorrow after I meet with the princess. It is essential that you wait for my return.* He heads away with short rapid steps to the main dwelling at the centre of the enclosure. The women summon the servants, add instructions to those previously formulated by Bwemba, then turn their back on Mutango, who finds himself not in their hands but in the care of the help. They take him to the smallest dwelling, to a room prepared for guests. There is a bare wooden bed, with a slightly tilted headrest and a broad-back chair. *Stranger,* they say, *we will bring you what you need for sustenance and for washing up before entering the night.*

Left alone, the man surveys the furniture looking for a mat but finds none. That he will have to make do with this bed bothers him. He has no idea how many others have rested their bodies there, to what dreams the irremovable headrest led their spirit. The Bwele are numerous, powerful and ingenious, but they still have much to learn about the laws that govern life. Not to take chances, he will use the furniture in an unorthodox way, with his feet on the headrest, his bag under his head like he did in the bush. Having resolved this question, Mutango circles the room slowly, examining every nook and cranny. Satisfied that there is nothing suspicious, he sits at the edge of the chair. The servants return. From outside, they ask permission to come in.

He gets up to open the door. Two young people, a boy and a girl whom he had not noticed before, are standing there. The girl is carrying a steaming dish of leaves and tubers in sauce. She is also carrying a jar filled with water. The boy hands him something that looks like a folded fabric. He is the one who speaks first, his lips turned down in a disapproving frown: *Stranger, let me freshen up your clothes tomorrow. You will leave them on the bed and put this on,* he says, presenting the fabric to him. His companion adds: *When you are finished eating, leave the plate in front of the door.* She steps into the room, place the plate and the jug by the chair, then says as she leaves: *We are next door. All you have to do is call. May the darkness be good to you.*

The door bangs shut on a thoughtful Mutango. The features of the two servants seem different from those of the Bwele he is used to meeting. They must come from one of the many regions of the country he has never visited. Admittedly, he is not overly concerned with the question. He is hungry, tired after having spent the whole night awake, having travelled in front of the day. Not surprising that, after his sleepless night, he could not walk as quickly as his companion. Disregarding the chair, he sits on the floor to eat his meal. As he dips his hand into the plate, the words come back to him, their echo filling the room: *Do not you know that the Bwele have cast their nets over us?* His stomach is rumbling. Yet he does not eat a bite, goes to wash his hand. He glances at his bag where he has only enough cured meat for the half-a-day journey back to his village. Not knowing what turn events will take, he chooses to keep the carefully chosen pieces of smoked monkey for later. He will not rest tonight either. It would not be safe to fall asleep when the spirits are commanding him not to trust the Bwele.

The earthen walls offer no openings to the outside, aside from the closed door. If he shuts his eyes, he will not even know that the sun has risen. Bwemba will not come looking for him before going to see the Princess Njole. The servants will not dare disturb his rest, the hunter's wives have no interest in his fate. The only solution is to stay awake once again. The fat man gets up, takes a few steps in the room, pricks up his ears in the hope of catching a noise on which his attention can focus. Nothing. He grabs the clothing he was given, starts unfolding it. Suddenly it occurs to him that he will not be noticed if he wears them. Some of the amulets he never removes might betray him but they will be barely noticeable from a distance, especially in a place where people are clad in particularly extravagant attire.

Mutango removes his manjua, ties the fabric around his large pelvis, decides, after a moment's reflection, not to leave his bag behind. Cautiously he opens the door, inspects the courtyard with a sharp eye, thinking all the while of what he will say if someone catches him by surprise: an urgent need. But no one is there. He steps outside, crosses the courtyard, heads to the main dwelling. Mutango circles the building entirely before finding the place where he will spend the night. He settles at a spot where no one will suspect his presence, out of sight of the three other houses. If, by misfortune, he does fall asleep, at least he will hear the hunter leaving his home.

*

A birdsong wakes him. He has slept like a baby, back against the side of the house, his game pouch in his arms. No doubt he has dreamt, probably several times. All has vanished. This is a bad sign in his community where it is thought that those who do not dream have ceased living. What worries him much more is the thought that he may have missed his host leaving. The sun has not yet found its place in the sky, dissipated the night shadows lingering like intangible yet very real presences. But this is not enough to reassure him. He knows the hunter will have set out before daybreak to meet with Princess Njole. His instinct tells him the meeting is important. He wonders how he can get into the royal domain, find the princess' quarters without being seen. He hears a creaking sound. His host calls a servant, asks for something to eat. Mutango, ready to spring behind the trees, waits from the man to go back inside.

Having inched forward, he catches sight of an attendant disappearing into the compound's smallest hut. Without a second thought, Mutango risks all for all, bounds to the exit. His pitiless feet leave a trail in the dust, as if two or three elephants were racing one another. By chance, the morning breeze rises, spinning particles of earth, erasing the formidable mark of his footprints. He has never run like this, at full tilt, the wind whistling in his ears, holding the bottom of his clothing in one hand. Once outside, he feels his heart rising to his throat, his lungs like empty sacs in his ribcage.

Reeling towards a thorny thicket along the path, the Mulongo notable tries his best to conceal his massive body and to catch his breath in silence. He pats his pouch, commends himself for not leaving it behind. His absence will soon be noticed. It will be taken as a slap in the face. His host bid him not to leave the compound before they saw each other. Mutango knows he will not be able to come back here. His few remaining pieces of cured monkey will be of great help. Right now, they are his only asset.

The town is still steeped in darkness when the hunter comes out. Dressed in the clothing of Bwele men, his waist is girded in beads and grains, the wide curved blade of a ceremonial knife hangs from his belt down to his right thigh. It shines with the lustre of a star fallen from the sky. Bwemba is also wearing a three-bladed throwing knife, with two curved blades. The smaller third blade is in the shape of an assegai tip. It is very close to the handle, leaving little room for the hand. Just holding such a weapon requires self-composure. Mutango remains unimpressed. He focuses his gaze on the leather strips crisscrossing the hunter's chest and back.

He lets Bwemba get a head start, follows hiding as best he can behind thickets and granaries. From the homes they pass, voices can be heard, the sound of kitchen utensils or the cries of children. The hunter stops at a compound surrounded by an enclosure which indicates the high status of the people who live there. But it is not the royal domain, of this the fat dignitary is sure. The house in front of which the hunter stands is next to a group of more ordinary homes. Mutango hesitates. Should he follow the man inside or wait for him to come out and continue on his way to the royal domain? Approaching the entrance, he observes something that intrigues him: the wall does not protect several homes but a single construction, relatively small, that could not house people of the upper caste.

There are no guards to be seen, no sign of torches with by-now-cooled embers that would have served for lighting at night. It seems as if no one lives here. The Mulongo notable slips cautiously into the court-yard. Bwemba knocks on the door, seems to say something, then retreats, goes around the building. Soon, a female silhouette appears. Mutango is too far to see her clearly but he understands that propriety forbids the princess and the hunter from meeting alone in a closed space. For honour's sake, they must meet out-doors. It is time to draw near, find out what is being planned.

The princess—for indeed it is she—is seated opposite the hunter. They are behind the house under an awning resting on tall pillars. There Bwemba gives an account so astonishing that Mutango must bite his tongue to keep from speaking up, hold his side to avoid leaping forward right there on the spot. *I did as agreed, your Highness*, says the hunter. *The Mulongo trade emissary wanted to know what became of the men we captured. He is a shrewd man. So he did not put the question to me in so many words, asking me instead if I had seen a column of men on our lands. I answered him.*

He gave me a cutlass and would have had me believe that the Minister of Rites had officiated over it. But he was lying. The woman nods: *So, we cannot put our trust in this individual to accomplish what we were planning. Now, why is he here?* The hunter shrugs. He had not expected the Mulongo notable to want to follow him. But the trade emissary got excited when he heard about the men with hen feet and seems to have taken some extravagant idea into his head.

The time has come for him to return to his village. It is pointless to try to see Queen Njanjo, who must know about all this. If he is going to undertake a journey to the coastal country, he cannot do so alone. It was crazy to even think of doing so. As he is about to turn back, he feels a sharp metal tip jabbing into his lower back. *Move it!* a woman's voice orders. He is pushed under the awning. At that very moment, all the incantations he has learnt, repeated so many times, escape him. Mutango feels nothing but his guts writhing from hunger, a single thought resonating within: *Do you not know that the Bwele cast their nets over us?*

Mukano and his personal guards left Mulongo territory first thing in the morning. The last traces of the night had barely dissipated when they set out on Mbenge road to Bwele county. Dusk interrupted their progress. They started out again at daybreak, eating little, hardly talking at all. As they approach Bwele

Léonora
Miano

100

territory, the tension becomes increasingly palpable. The town of Bekombo is not yet visible but they will reach it soon, when the sun is at its zenith. The chief feels prey to an anxiety that makes his steps heavy. He tries to concentrate on details: the value of the gifts chosen for Queen Njanjo, what he will say once he is in her presence. The men in the front stop abruptly. He is about to admonish them when he sees why.

A column of Bwele warriors is barring their way. The one in command is wearing a head covering with a long visor, studded with beads. He issues a simple order, in a peremptory tone: *Arrest them!* Mukano reminds them of his rank, of the improper character of such behaviour towards peaceful neighbours. Nothing comes of all his protests. He and his men are stripped of their weapons and the gifts they brought for Njanjo. Shackled, they are told to advance. At least they are not gagged. *Queen's orders* is the only response to his objections. The chief of the Mulongo clan cannot understand what forces are at work for him to be treated this way. Did he commit an offence? Is this a punishment from Nyambe for having taken so much time to look for the men who are missing from his community? Tears run down his high cheekbones. He does not hear the comments of the Bwele population when he and his men arrive in Bekombo: the teenagers jeer, the young children ask their mother questions. None of this reaches his ears.

They are led to the royal domain. A special meeting was held in the morning. Dignitaries from all regions of the county are still there. When the Mulongo prisoners enter the vast compound where the queen and her entourage reside, they see Mutango, on his knees. His back and calves are covered in blood, his face in bruises. Women with bows and quivers surround him as Princess Njole addresses the assembly: *This man was taken at daybreak. He had stolen into the archers' residence. We think he is a spy sent by our neighbours. We have interrogated him. So far, he has not confessed. I put guards on the roads to our territory in case others come unannounced.* As far as the Bwele are concerned, nothing more needs be said. The Mulongo are ill-intentioned. Mukano is nonetheless given the chance to speak up. He refuses to do so as long as he is in shackles. There is nothing his people have ever done to justify such treatment. He does not look at his brother who pleads with him: *In the name of all that binds us, tell these people I have done nothing wrong!* The fat man's voice is but a frail breath.

Head high, the Mulongo chief looks straight ahead at Queen Njanjo, the only person in his eyes worthy to hear his words. He came to meet with her. If these moments are the last of his reign, he intends to behave like a janea to the bitter end. Let it not be said when the story is passed down to future genera-tions that Mukano bowed to injustice. Let it not be said that he stood before the queen of the Bwele and did not dare question her about the fate of the twelve missing men. The Mulongo chief waits. His men model their attitude on his. Silent, they stand with their feet firmly on the ground, lift their heads high.

Not one looks down at Mutango who continues to moan.

Njanjo rises. She is a small woman, but her authority is such that no one would think of challenging it. She wears a beaded head covering, framing her face and tied at the chin. With a wave of the hand she orders her people to remove the fetters from her Mulongo homologue and his entourage. *You are welcome here Mukano*, she says. *Pardon my soldiers. They were just heeding the instructions of my sister Njole.* The man nods his head, spurns the seat offered to him and, still standing, gets straight to the point: *Njanjo, it has been a long time since I have come here in person. I hoped for a different welcome, even though, it is true, I did not announce my visit by sending you a messenger as is customary . . .* The queen interrupts him. *Do you swear*, she asks pointing to Mutango, *that you did not send him to spy on us?*

For the first time, Mukano looks at his brother. Without batting an eyelid, he replies: *He came here without informing me. I know nothing of his motives.* Njanjo asks: *Do you authorize us to bring him before our courts of justice?* Mukano is silent. Images race through his mind. He sees his brother's wrongdoing over the years, his scheming, his misdeeds even on the night of the great fire when he found him sleeping with one of his own daughters. This memory disgusts him. The act is so serious that its perpetrator should have been banished, a punishment that Mutango would have escaped only because of his rank. The Mulongo chief's voice is powerful and clear when he declares: *Do with him as you see fit.*

It takes eight warriors under Njole's command to carry off the accused who struggles, yells that the ancestors will not permit such an infamy. Mukano remains calm, keeps himself from replying that the ancestors are tired; they have had enough of his brother's misconduct; he is only getting what is coming to him. Once the archers are gone, Njanjo orders Mukano's staff of command to be returned to him. *Now,* she appeals to him, *please take a seat.* If he does not sit down, the Mulongo chief will be offending his host, which is not advisable. She claps. *First we will have something to eat. My advisors and I have had much to do since sunrise and we still have not eaten anything.* The chief takes advantage of the moment to have his gifts placed at the foot of the queen's seat of authority. His men take them back from the soldiers. But the customary words are not pronounced. The usual blessings are not uttered. Njanjo does not rhapsodize over the objects she has been given. Nothing happens in accordance with time-honoured rules.

*

In his prison, Mutango is seething with rage. His anger is so intense, he cannot even think about finding a way out. The severity of the shock made him forget the slightest incantation. The contents of his pouch were tossed at him. Bwele do not eat monkey. *You are really savages,* one of the warriors says to him. *We should subjugate you to teach you the proper way to live. We would have done so already, I think, if your lands were not so inaccessible during rainy season. Travel must be possible between all regions of the country.* Mutango is stretched out on the ground. Every inch of his body hurts. Hunger clouds his mind. He tries nonetheless to remember the events of recent days to figure out where he went wrong. In vain.

Something eludes him, he knows not what. His still-open eye—the other is severely swollen—scans the dark room whose ceiling is so low he cannot stand up. A smell of urine floats in the air mingled with the odour of the meatless leaf sauce he was served. The woman who brought it to him said, *Eat. We do not want you to die.* Then what do they want? He would rather die than find out. If he could have imagined when he walked into this compound at daybreak that it housed a garrison of soldiers—a sacrilegious species of women if ever there was one—he would no doubt have headed home. From the time his presence was detected, his life has been a nightmare. If these women do not kill him, he has everything to fear.

Unrelenting thoughts are whirling through his mind when a voice breaks through: *Son of Mulongo, I will not ask you how you have left the night. It is unlikely that you will ever leave it again. Our archers are going to cast you into darkness for all eternity. Hence you deserve one last present from me. If you have any questions, I am ready to reply.* Bwemba is standing in the doorway. Mutango does not think for a moment of thrusting him aside, of running out. He would not be able to take a single step before the women pounced on him. His healthy eye passes over the visitor. It is not only because he is on the ground that the hunter looks bigger. It is because Bwemba has been a step ahead from the start. No, he will not ask him anything. He closes his eye. But the hunter feels like talking. His arms crossed, a smile on his lips, he tells of the night of the great fire, describes the operation carried out by his men while the Mulongo were sleeping. It was not hard to set the homes on fire. They were so rudimentary, with their roofs of dried lende leaves, their wooden pillars.

The Bwele had a good laugh, seeing their neighbours scurrying like insects. He himself was there when twelve Mulongo men were captured. They were dozing in the bush, did not suspect a thing. They were not brought here to Bekomo. They were led instead on other paths along the edge of Bwele country to the coast. They had to walk several long nights before reaching their destination. During the day, the abducted men were kept in the bush shelters that the Bwele built on the paths leading from one region to another of their territory, all the way to the coastal country. There the Mulongo men were handed over to the Coastlander princes. They delivered them in turn to the foreigners who have come across the waters from pongo. *We have no choice*, Bwemba explains. *To avoid open conflict with the Coastlanders, we must provide them with men. We reached an agreement with them because they were terrorizing some of our regions in an attempt to round up captives for the men with hen feet.*

He falls silent, takes a few steps forward and, standing close to Mutango, adds in a low voice: *Your brother did nothing to get you out of this bind. Rest assured, you will soon be avenged. We will let him go back to your lands. We will not wait before striking again. If war breaks out with the Mulongo, we will come out victorious. Then it will be easy to do what we please. As the chief, Mukano may be sacrificed. It has not been decided yet. Some think he should simply be handed over to the Coastlanders since he never attacked us. Others consider that a ritual killing would be a way of paying tribute to him—we do not sacrifice people of no importance, as you know. Regardless, you will stay here. After all, you chose to come.* The hunter smiles. *Anyway, you are too fat to be turned over to them. You would take up the space of three men in the vessels of the foreigners who have come across the waters from pongo. You are no gift to anyone.* With a shoulder-shaking outburst of laughter the hunter concludes: *Our archers are going to castrate you or cut out your tongue if they are feeling merciful. They are experts at wielding a cutlass. Once your wounds are healed, you will be in their service. A new life is starting for you. Try not to waste it.*

Bwemba takes his leave. The queen will soon be hearing the man with hen feet who ventured into Bwele country in the company of a few Coastlanders. It is the first time such a thing has happened. He is looking forward to seeing the foreigner whose skin has been coloured to make him look human. The Bwele have no access to the ocean but one day perhaps they will deal directly with the men who have come across the waters from pongo. He is anxious to know what will be said later at the audience, breaks out in laughter at the thought that the Coastlanders are taking the risk of losing their privileged position. Mutango wants to cry out; to think that he was willing to side with the Bwele against his own brother! He would like to implore them to put an end to his days. He shuts his eyes, tries to summon up the sacred words that would allow him to leave his body, send his spirit travelling somewhere, anywhere. There is nothing left in him; the magic words have vanished. The man is nothing but suffering flesh.

*

Mukano has still learnt nothing about the missing when he sets foot in his village again. His men have taken an oath not to pronounce his brother's name. No one will know they have left him to his fate. They have no compunction about this. The clan will finally be rid of a wicked force, the chief will have a free hand to govern. Mukano convokes the Council, informs them of his meeting with Queen Njanjo. The Bwele sovereign spoke. She declared she knew nothing of the clan's missing sons. They did not pass through Bwele territory, of this she is sure. Bwele country is perfectly administered. It is inconceivable that a group of strangers could have travelled through it without being noticed.

On the other hand, Njanjo informed him that footprints of a column of men were detected in the bush, between Bwele and Mulongo territory. Their trackers followed them for a while to make sure they did not signal danger, they went in the direction of jedu. They did not attempt to find out more. *It is my conviction*, Mukano declares to the gathered sages, *that we should head out in that direction to find our sons and brothers. Whatever the force that prompted them to go that way, it will return them to us.* This time the elders do not object. Mutango has not returned, his followers do not have the courage in his absence to stand up to the chief.

The janea's soldiers go to prepare a search party. The elders insist they do not set out without seeking protection from the spirits. Two days and two nights will be devoted to rituals and prayers. The chief asks the son of the spiritual guide, as inexperienced as he may be, to take charge of these operations. The midwife must also be informed as must the women whose sons they are seeking. They will come to the village square where the whole population will gather. Then they will be invited to return to their homes if they so desire. The separation has lasted too long already. *I want their sons*, the chief concludes, *to find them waiting on the threshold of the family compound when we bring them back.*

Mukano intends to participate in the search himself. Who better than a chief can embody the clan's motto—*I am because we are*—their guiding adage since the day when Queen Emene led her followers there, founded a new people? For the janea, the saying is not open to question. He is not proud of himself for having waited this long before looking for the men who went missing the night of the great fire. He wavered as if it were conceivable to abandon his own blood to the unknown, to silence. He too will submit to the directive given to the warriors not to come before the clan without a clear answer as to the fate of the missing.

Water Trails

The day the chief and his personal guards set out to Bwele country, the woman leaves the village. Slipping into the interstice between night and dawn, she precedes them, walking fearlessly on trails that are not there, that take shape under the soles of her feet, forming a road that is hers alone, like life's path. She is on her way. Nothing and no one has the power to stop her. A bag held by a strap across her forehead hangs down her back. She put provisions in it and some water in a sealed gourd. Another sack containing an earth-filled pot thumps against her right side. Eyabe does not wonder which way to go. Something drives her, leads her. The love of a mother for her child has no need for stars to find its way. It is itself the guiding star.

The woman feels at peace. When she gets there, she will recognize the place where she will scatter the earth from under the dikube, honour with dignity the spirit of her firstborn and his companions. It will take the time it takes. She walks. Her breath merges with the breath of the wind. She is at one with nature, moves without stirring a single branch of shrub, takes care not to crush the small inhabitants that live here: the larvae, caterpillars or insects nestled in the grass. If she inadvertently touches them, she humbly asks forgiveness, continues on her way. All that lives harbours a spirit. All that lives manifests the divine. When night falls, she no longer sees well enough to continue. She stops, puts down her bags, finds a tree stump to serve as a headrest, falls asleep. In her dreams, her son's voice speaks to her of the land of water.

It is not a wet land, he says. *Here, water is the land. It is the sky and the wind.* Eyabe does not doubt any of this. She has confidence, does not count the passing days. She walks in the direction of jedu. The stories told in her village say nothing about this part of Creation. They speak only of the great voyage of Queen Emene from pongo to mikondo, to where the Mulongo now live; as for the land where they once lived, no one knows anything any more. They speak only of Bwele territory in mbenge. No one in Eyabe's clan is familiar with the path she is taking. It is not inaccessible; she travels it easily. When her feet begin to sink into muddy earth, she thinks it is for this reason that no one comes here. A smell of moisture rises from the earth, like after heavy rainfall. Eyabe knows this is not the land of water, the place where she will scatter the earth where her son's plant-double grew.

Now that she thinks of it, the fall of the tree seems to be one more sign confirming the end of her son's passage on earth. Is the land of water a world beyond? How many other dimensions are there to receive souls that have left the world of the living? Is it possible to be reincarnated if one is resting at the bottom of the water? It is likely she will never know. Continuing on her way, she wonders where she will spend another night far from the clan. The fifth or sixth, she knows not, nor does she care. Hearing the soft suck of the mud under her feet, she need not examine the ground to see that it is impossible to lie down. Should she climb to rest atop one of the trees with visible roots? The risk of falling is too great. The many branches also look too fragile to bear the weight of a human body. Eyabe tries not to lose her composure. She must remain confident. She is growing tired. She presses on. Mud is covering her calves, weighing down the hems of her manjua but she plods on. She is struck by severe itching on the soles of her feet but, having no idea what lives down in the marsh, she does not dare scratch. To keep from being overwhelmed by anxiety, she recalls her final moments in the village.

The women whose sons were missing had fallen asleep after having kept vigil all night. Seated around her feverish body, they listened attentively, hearing the voice that, passing through her, told a sad story. It spoke of separation, violence and powerlessness. It spoke of the impossibility of coming back, of a death that was not death since it may not allow for rebirth. An incomplete death. Everlasting solitude. The silence of the spirits although they were entreated relentlessly. The women whose sons went missing swore not to spread the word in the community. Even the women who had no desire to see their offspring again felt heavy-hearted. They did not love their child any better than before but they realized that he was a part of them. Not only a body that chose them as a passageway. Not only the flesh of their flesh. Some of the women cut their hair. Others did not dare. All of them laid their bodies down, drained, exhausted.

Only the midwife was with Eyabe when she left. They walked together to the edge of Mulongo territory, careful not to draw the attention of the guards who were about to leave their post. The latter are supposed to wait for the new guards to arrive before going home, but they seldom do. They are having a hard time getting used to the security measures taken after the great fire. They stand guard every night but nothing happens. Their attention diminishes; they take liberties, hurry to get home when night-time is coming to an end, even though the daylight has not yet found its place, neither on the earth nor in the sky. They walked without exchanging a word. Everything had been said. The elder had placed her right hand on Eyabe's forehead and, calling the blessing of the spirits down on her, had given Eyabe her shield. They held each other briefly, then Ebeise rushed back to tell the women in the communal hut about the departure of their companion. Wading through the bog, Eyabe wonders how the midwife presented her departure, what she said to make sure that no one would betray them, that no one would go to the Council and say: *One of us has gone off to look for the land of water, the final resting place of our sons.*

A painful cramp grips her right thigh, making her stop for a moment. She stifles a moan and, with the flat of her hand, wipes the sweat pouring down her forehead. She must be the victim of an hallucination, she thinks, when she sees her there, motionless. A few steps away, a young girl is standing on the trunk of a tree that has been thrown across the path. They look at each other for a moment, then the child scampers away, disappears as quickly as she had appeared. Eyabe does not feel she can make it to the tree trunk which seems very real. The ground is slipping away beneath her feet; her head is spinning. A murmur reaches her, she thinks, but is not sure.

Everything grows dark. Her last meal was long ago. It was impossible to stop in the middle of the marsh, set her bag down on the ground to eat. Her legs refuse to budge. She is going to die right here, standing in the muddy earth, without having approached the land of water. Did she interpret the signs correctly? The words she received during her trance? Eyabe brings her hand to her bosom, clutches with trembling fingers the amulet the midwife gave her. Her intuitions may have misled her but they could not have deceived the midwife. Eyabe waits. Standing. She waits. For something. For someone.

*

The sun has changed names several times. Its brightness has subsided by the time the girl comes back. Still silent, she points to the woman whose feet are mired in mud. Faces appear behind her, faces whose bodies Eyabe cannot see. They emerge from the surrounding foliage like large buds amid greenery. A mouth seems to open and close but Eyabe hears nothing. Unwittingly, she stretches her neck, realizes they are talking to her. She does not understand the language but she is the one being addressed. Should she shake or nod her head, she does not know, so she smiles as best she can, gestures to her legs sunk in the mud, tells them, in her own language, that she cannot move.

No one on the other side stirs in her direction. Faces retreat behind the plants and disappear. Only the child stays there on the tree trunk. Her big black eyes study the stranger. Without having noticed any movement around her, Eyabe becomes conscious of the presence of two men by her side. They have come up from behind, thrown on the ground a raft of branches assembled with creepers and ribs. One of them wields a long pole with which he pushes the platform forward. His companion removes the woman's pack, places it on the raft. Then he works to pull Eyabe towards him, holds her shoulders firmly, speaks in a low voice words she does not understand. It is his gaze that enlightens her. She imitates his gesture, feels the power of his body drawing her out of the mud. He presses her to him, whispering words whose music soothes her.

When her feet touch the wood, her knees buckle. They go back along the path the men took to reach her. The mud gives way to a stream, then a river.

Eyabe has never seen such a big waterway. But her heart tells her this is not yet the place where she must go. When she sees it, she will know. Inwardly, she thanks the spirit of the ancestors. It is because they interceded with Nyambe on her behalf that these people were sent to her. She does not know their language but she can feel their energy. When they reach the riverbank, the girl is there. Women are also present. A community lives here, a few days walk towards jedu from Mulongo territory.

Rafts float gently along the banks of the water. They are made of three layers of solidly attached branches. Some are tied to a stake driven into the muddy ground on the riverside. When the backwash takes them out, the rope stretches slightly and tugs them back ashore. Two small boys, kneeling on the embankment, thrust their hands into the water. Laughing they pull out animals with glistening skin. She has never seen anything like this in Mulongo country. The newcomer observes them at length, sees them tossing their wriggling catch into a basket. She watches in silence, surprised at the sight of this animal that does not cry out.

They help her ashore. She is left in the company of two women. Each has put one of the stranger's arms around her shoulder. She feels their skin on hers. The contact revives her strength. The earth is not as muddy as the ground that held her prisoner but it is surprisingly wet, as if it had rained for days on end. The women accompanying her walk cautiously. The huts of this community are built at a distance from the river, away from the shore. They stand on pillars buried deep in the ground, rise to what seems to Eyabe like incongruous heights, before one can see the floor. The woman wonders how people get up to these dwellings, why they had to be raised like this.

They stop in front of a house on stilts. One of her companions points to a ladder, indicates with gestures and words how to climb up to go inside. Eyabe thinks this is out of the question. The air fills with laughter. That they are inviting her to try, she understands from their intonations. They clap to encourage her, improvise a song. Just as she is wondering whether the spirits are really on her side, a face appears in the doorway to the hut. Someone speaks to her in her language: *Woman, the water is rising. Soon the earth will disappear. If you stay there, no one will be able to do anything for you. Night is coming.* Eyabe utters a long cry; she recognizes Mutimbo, one of the two older men who vanished in the company of the ten young initiates after the great fire. Too many emotions, too many words collide inside her, make her tremble, lose consciousness.

*

Mutimbo is there when she opens her eyes. She does not realize that she blacked out for a whole day. It is evening. No fire has been kindled to provide light. Even though the swamp makes access to the village very difficult, the inhabitants still avoid anything that could draw attention to its existence. The waters have risen, as always at this time of day. This is what he tells her when she enquires about the noise she is hearing. *It is the water*, he replies smiling. *I told you it would soon flood the world.* The waves thump against the stilts at a steady rhythm until, having reached a certain level, the lapping of the water becomes a whisper. Eyabe feels like she is hearing the song of Weya, the original earth. This troubles her a little. Since she set out to find the land of water, she has considered it a hostile power, the harmful force that robbed her of her firstborn. The one whose coming into the world consecrated her femininity in the clan's eyes. The one who enabled her to know herself as she had never imagined she could be. Inventive: oh, the many melodies that came to mind when he needed to be lulled to sleep. Knowing: for she had an answer to his questions, if not always, then often. Gentle: and this after an adolescence spent rivalling her brothers at sling-shooting and shunning basketry, the interest of which she never understood. From this turbulent period, she has kept her lean muscular body.

Eyabe has always been a woman inhabited by a man's spirit. The lovers of her youth never took exception to this trait; neither did the man who married her. At times during their lovemaking, her husband would remind her with a twinkle in his eye: *You do know that I am the man?* To which she replied: *I would not have agreed to marry you otherwise. But know that I too am the man. When the divine fashioned the human being, she breathed both energies into us.* When Eyabe became an expert hairstylist, it was because she never thought of it as a job for women only. To the Mulongo, a person's coiffure is equally important to men and women. They all come to her because she is said to have an able hand. Seeing her husband Musinga's face dancing in her memory, she chases it out of her mind. He did not come to visit her in the communal hut. She wants nothing to do with him any more.

The village seems so far away. It was Etina when she left the clan's territory.

After a while, she stopped counting the days, stopped naming them. Time has not vanished into thin air; it is still there. It has simply lost its meaning. What does it matter how much time has gone by since her son will not be returned to her; she will never see him again as she knew him before. She will never see him take a woman. Become a father. The soft glow of twilight is all that filters through the log walls. Two other people are in the hut, their presence barely perceptible. Her eyes adjust to the half-light, cling to the man. For her, there is no one here but him and all the things she would like to ask him. When he draws near the mat where Eyabe is resting, she notices that he is wearing only an eyobo over his loins, that he is walking with difficulty. Mutimbo has a stiff leg.

The poultice applied to his nasty wound makes it hard for him to wear anything more elaborate. He winces as he approaches but soon the expression of pain melts into a smile. *I prayed so*, he says. *The spirits heard me. So many times I thought I was going to die without seeing anyone from our clan, anyone who I could tell, someone who could tell the others. As you can see, it will take time before I can go back to the village.* Mutimbo speaks of the great fire, the night when the face of the world changed. He tells her what she knows and also what she could not have imagined. That nocturnal shadows were still in the sky when Bwele men cast their hunting nets over them. *I was with Mundene̲ and our sons in the bush.* In the blink of an eye, they were gagged, shackled, dragged far from Mulongo territory. He does not recall crying out or hearing his companions do so. It did not occur to them. Or maybe it did. He does not know any more. They were still in the throes of despondency that weighed on their spirits since the fire.

It all occurred as in a dream. It was not real. It could not be happening to us. We were going to wake up. Take stock of the disaster caused by the great fire. Gird ourselves with valour to rebuild. Honour our ancestors since lives had not been lost. At least the fire had spared lives. So we would live. We had not survived the fire only to face another ordeal. It was not real. It could not be happening to us. We were going to wake up. Take stock of the disaster caused by the great fire. Gird ourselves with valour. Rebuild. We were alive.

Since he arrived here Mutimbo has been asking himself why he and his companions kept walking. Why, if they could not fight, had they chosen to keep going rather than let themselves be killed. This question was already gnawing at him after three and a half days of marching. That is why he ceased walking, tried to urge his companions to stop too. The Bwele did not give him the time. One of them shot him with an arrow, so deeply it pierced the flesh of his groin. They unshackled him, left him behind, convinced that a wild animal, drawn to the smell of blood, would do him in. He had no idea where he was or in which direction the village was. *Anyway, I was in no condition to go back. I was losing a lot of blood. I said we walked three and half days but that was not exactly the case.*

In fact, they travelled at night. Only at night. During the day, they were kept in shelters built by the Bwele deep in a heart of the bush which grew thicker and darker even in broad daylight. After a while, they forgot the radiance of the sun, saw only the shadow, moonless nights, holed up in hovels designed for their confinement. They could not tell what direction they had taken or where they were situated. The Bwele had shaved their heads and the beards of the men who had hair on their faces—the two older men—to make them look like prisoners of war in case they were seen. They stripped them of their amulets, adornments and clothes. *If they could have rid us of our scarifications, I think they would have.* They were fettered with ropes around their wrists. Two branches of mwenge, skilfully tied together, were placed on their shoulders, so that they could barely move their heads. All they could see was the nape of the neck of the person in front of them. It was impossible to communicate. The mwenge, known for its hardness, lacerated their skin at the slightest twisting of the neck.

Mutimbo had stopped walking at a specific point in time. While mulling once again, as so many times before, over the reasons why he and his companions did not offer more resistance, even at the cost of their lives, he overheard the Bwele whispering to each other. One was complaining about Queen Njanjo's orders. She had forbidden moving the columns of captives during the day. The other answered that there were several reasons for this. First, they did not want to bump into anyone meddlesome. Second, it worked to deprive the detainees of all bearings. Finally, it accustomed them to the shadows. *He said, I'll never forget his words: 'Where we are taking them, there is only darkness. Permanently. They have to be prepared.'* The man knew nothing more, was just following orders. Mutimbo was the only one to hear this exchange. He never had the chance to let his brothers know. The last image he has is of them being pushed forward, the Bwele cursing, threatening, brandishing their throwing knives, pointing their poison arrows at them. *They were armed to the teeth. It would have taken them no time to finish us off.* Mulongo culture forbids the taking of one's own life. An act of resistance in such conditions would have been suicidal. An insult to the ancestors, to the maloba. An offence to Nyambe, the Creator, who divided up his own energy to spread it and thus live in all things.

I suppose this is why we walked on. Against our will. Without knowing where we were going. I suppose. We did not speak much, even when we were in the shelters. Some of the Bwele know our language. Our young initiates whispered encouragements to each other to hold out until the time was ripe. Mundene, our Minister of Rites, never stopped cursing our assailants, calling on our forefathers. Our capture was an act of cowardice. It was also a transgression: we had committed no crime, done nothing wrong. We were not given the chance to confront our enemies in a fair fight. They had no right to deprive us of our freedom. Our assailants never untied our wrists, not even to eat or to relieve ourselves. The time was never ripe. And would we have known to seize it? A few days of utter humiliation is all it takes to crush a fighting spirit. As time went by, we were less and less ourselves. One of our boys began to defy the spirits, refused to eat despite the blows. He, no doubt, died on the way.

In a low voice, Eyabe asks who this young man was: *Whose child?* she asks. *If my memory serves me well, it was Ebusi's son,* he replies. The woman nods her head slowly, suppressing the sob that wells up in her chest at the thought of her companion in isolation. The only other woman among the outcasts to have dared to leave the communal hut. Should she take it as a sign? Could it be that only Ebusi and her son passed away? If one perished for having resisted his assailants by refusing to eat, how did the other one die? The words that came to her seemed to indicate that several of the clan's sons had entered the land of water. She does not know what to think, shuts her eyes when Mutimbo exhorts her to go back to the village to explain to the chief and the Council that the Bwele are responsible for the disappearance of the twelve Mulongo men.

He wants her to go find his wife Eleke. *She must know I am alive. We have never been apart more than a day.* Eyabe does not know what to do any more. She listens to Mutimbo, who describes how he came to this community that has protected and cared for him. She learns that these welcoming people are not really a people, in the usual sense of the term. They do not share a common memory. Their clan has neither founder nor ministering ancestors. They have all brought their own individual totems, beliefs, methods of healing. All this, put together in a common pot of sorts, forms a spirituality to which they all adhere. The men and women divide up the tasks in a clear, simple way: the men hunt, fish, safeguard the physical integrity of the community; the women grow crops, take charge of the interior life. They all work together to build the dwellings. There is no reigning lineage. The community chose for itself a chief that it can dismiss if the person does not live up to their expectations.

When Eyabe asks about this system of organization, Mutimbo explains: *The people who live here have fled from the attacks of the Coastlanders and their henchmen.* The people who call themselves children of the water are sowing terror everywhere within their reach, sparing only those villages inhabited by sister communities. The latter serve as intermediaries for bringing captives from inland regions. They head out on their pirogues, ambush anyone who ventures into the ocean in the areas around their village. They cross the fiefs of friendly tribes, thus reach the places where the capture is conducted. It takes time, sometimes a whole moon, to bring their prisoners to the coast. As a result, assistance from friendly tribes is indispensable. Only the distance and the impassable terrain keeps them from coming to Bebayedi to dislodge the inhabitants of the houses on stilts. In the end, Mutimbo does not understand all the workings of this complex system. All he knows is that the fate of the abducted is sealed in the coastal country. *But why are these people being torn away from their* *homes?* chokes Eyabe, who cannot believe what she is hearing. All this is beyond anything she could have imagined.

Mutimbo shrugs. He has heard it said that the Coastlander princes were allied with the strangers with hen feet. *They do not really have hen feet but they wear clothes on their legs that give this impression. I was told that the Coastlanders have been trading for a long time with these foreigners who came across the waters from pongo. From what I have understood, they used to supply them with red oil and elephant tusks. Now they give them people, even children, in exchange for merchandise. It seems the Coastlanders now have a reed that spits fire, shoots deadly projectiles. The men with hen feet supplied these to them to help them subjugate their captives.*

Lest they be decimated by those wielding fire who can kill from afar, the communities under attack have begun retreating inland to places where untamed nature offers protection. That is how this village came to be, surrounded as it is by a river and swamps. It is not easy to enter the enclave without being spotted. The people living here come from different places. Some, from territories conquered by the Bwele, have refused to become subjects of Queen Njanjo. Understandably so, considering she demands a human tribute from her vassals. This is how the Bwele became the Coastlanders' most important intermediaries in the trade of human beings. After all, the Bwele have dominion over more territory than the Coastlander princes, who have only managed to gain ascendancy through cunning and cruelty. Be that as it may, the Bwele do not want to make enemies of them. Only the Coastlanders have fire power.

Eyabe covers her mouth with both hands to keep from crying out, from yelling that the world has gone mad, that dark forces are at work, that even a newborn could readily recognize the face of witchcraft, that there could be no need for so many human lives, unless it is to sacrifice them to evil powers. Her heart races in her chest. It pounds with such fury that she feels she will burst asunder. This seems to her a happier prospect than living in a world where things like what Mutimbo is describing can happen. Horrified, she lets him continue, her eyes flowing over with tears. The man tells her that the different people who make up the population of this village, lost in the heart of the swamp, feel safe here. The Bwele will not venture out this far; they are forbidden by their faith to approach these water-soaked lands. They can go to the coast but will avoid marshes like this. The terrain is uncomfortable but they have learnt to live here. They now know how to build huts on stilts, fish in the river, hunt in the surrounding bush. The children know how to find shellfish, tease them out of the holes in the bog. The adults know which plants are edible, which are poisonous, which can be used for medicinal purposes. The language is a mix of all the tongues that came together on this muddy ground.

Smiling weakly, Mutimbo tells her that he has added some Mulongo words to their common language, especially to describe elements of the wickerwork that the women are learning to do thanks to him. Due to his disability he cannot journey out in the bush like the other men. So he stays with the women. Eyabe interrupts him. Something in what he says has struck her. Never before has she heard anyone speak about a coast or an ocean. She asks Mutimbo who explains that he himself is not sure what these terms refer to. *I mean I do not know concretely since I have never seen them with my own eyes. The coast is the place where the earth ends. The ocean is the territory that starts there, at the edge of the world and that is made up entirely of water.—The ocean then is the land of water?* Eyabe asks. Mutimbo remains thoughtful for a moment before nodding his head: *Yes, I think one can say that. The ocean is the land of water.—And these strangers, the men with hen feet, from what territory . . .—Now, my child, you are asking too much,* he replies. *I have only heard it said that they come across the ocean from pongo.*

*

Night falls abruptly, like an overripe fruit. It comes crashing down over the swamp, the river, the huts built on stilts. The darkness has a texture, the texture of kasimangolo flesh whose sweet flavour can be tasted only by cautiously sucking the prickles of the pit. Night is made for rest, but it is not peaceful. One must stay alert. The night has a smell, the smell of the skin of people who are together by force of circumstance. People who would never have met if they had not had to flee, run without knowing where they were going to save their lives, to find a new life. The night smells of memories that the day holds at bay because the people keep themselves busy assembling the parts of a hut on stilts, hunting, pounding, scaling, caring for newborns, caressing the cheek of an infant who does not speak, finding a name for him to keep him in the family of men. The night stirs up memories of the last day of a former life, in a previous world, on one's native soil. When one thinks of it, one has the feeling it all happened in a different reality. When one thinks of it, it is possible that one recalls many attacks. This one was not the first . . .

In any case, night revives the cries, the fears, the moment when you were alone on the road, the instant when a loved one fell never to rise again. There was no time to bury him. No time to invoke the maloba. It is a sin not to perform the rituals. It is like leaving an obstacle on the passage of the deceased. At night, you see the lifeless body again. The mouth that will smile no more, will call no more. You think of the soul that wanders because the mourning ceremonies were not held. At night, you remember that you had an occupation, a place in the community. You were just initiated. Respected. About to take a wife. About to name a firstborn in a ceremony of presentation to the ancestors. At night, you remember that you belonged to an inferior caste, were used for anything and everything from morning to night, interminably, that you were not in charge of your own life. Escaping to the unknown could not be worse than this. You took to the road oblivious to the cost. So often, you had thought of breaking free. Never had you given freedom the drawn features of the wounded brother you had had to leave behind. You ran without a backward glance, tears pouring from your eyes. You felt his eyes on your back and, in your heart, the piercing sound of his call, the silence after his voice broke down. Night becomes a descent, not so much into the darkness that protects gestations as into impenetrable gloom, into that which is produced by the folly of men.

They shared a frugal meal. Fish, boiled roots, bitter leaves. Eyabe never had fish before. She knows now that she does not like it. The awful smell drives away any desire to taste it. The reek of the raw fish is so bad it leaves a lasting impression, even after it has been dissipated by seasoning and cooking. At any rate, the woman would rather not eat the flesh of animals before accomplishing her mission. Mutimbo is still in the hut when night settles in. It is hard for him to leave the place. This dwelling, the very first upon arrival in the marshlands of the community, accommodates newcomers and the sick. In many cases, the people here are both. Mutimbo has never slept anywhere else. He cannot say when he was first brought here. Some men had gone to check their traps not far from the village. They found him lying nearly lifeless across the path. That he had dragged his body over the ground could be seen from the trail of blood he left. *I was delirious when they discovered me. They carried me here.* He later learnt that it was not the first time they had picked up a wounded man in the bush. They knew what he had escaped from.

Eyabe looks around but cannot discern the other faces. A moment ago, it seemed to her that a pregnant woman was resting in a corner. She did not see the other person. She asks Mutimbo who the occupants are. *There were three of us before you came.* There is indeed a woman about to give birth. And also a boy. He is mute. He had hidden at the bottom of a pit when the Coastlanders attacked his people. When he came out, only he and an old man were left. The old man did not survive the journey through the bush. He did not have the time to explain where the two came from. No one knows what people engendered the little one. Judging from his scarifications and his hair, some think he is a native of the coastal country where he must have belonged to the servant caste, former captives who were now subjects. Others argue that he would have a cut ear if that were the case, this amputation being a distinctive sign of the vanquished in coastal territory. No one knows for sure. The land where the earth ends is a very long walk from here. The quickest way to get there is to travel down the Kwa river that runs through the bush before flowing into the ocean. Even by way of the river, it takes days to reach the limits of Creation.

Every time she hears the word ocean, Eyabe̱'s heart pounds. *Man, I cannot go home,* she says. *I realize our people must learn as soon as possible to be on their guard against the Bwele, but . . .* She falls silent. Now is not the time to speak of the shadow that blocked out the light of day over the communal hut, the revelations that were made to her on the eve of her departure. Mutimbo nods, does not get angry, does not try to convince her. He knows she did not defy all the prohibitions of leaving the village without having a good reason. He will wait for her to reveal them to him, will pray unceasingly for the Mulongo to be spared.

*

Eyabe̱ can barely take it all in. She has just heard confirmation that, as she always thought, the world is not limited to the Mulongo and the Bwele, even though she knows there are a great many of the latter. Her steps led her to this place, called Bebayedi, where a new people has found shelter, a place whose name evokes at once parting and beginning, rupture and birth. Bebayedi is a genesis. The people here have different ancestors, different languages. Yet they now form a whole. They fled from thunder and fury. Sprang from chaos, refusing to be dragged into a life whose meaning was out of their hands, to be snatched by a death without knowing its finality and modalities. And so, without a blueprint, they brought a world into being. If they manage to stay alive, they will spawn generations. They themselves will take on the status of ancestors; they will bequeath a language composed of several others, forms of worship forged through a fusion of beliefs. They may survive the horrors of man hunting man, described by Mutimbo, but then so will their assailants. What will the space inhabited by humans look like under the reign of distrust? How will people live with their hearts full of bitter memories? In such an environment, the Mulongo will no longer trade with the Bwele. They will not travel the distance to the marsh behind the tanda to find a peaceable people. And if they came, if they arrived in great numbers, perhaps the people of Bebayedi would not be as friendly as they were to a woman alone, exhausted by days of walking through the bush.

She thinks of the ocean, tries to picture it, gives up on the idea. And yet she feels certain of one thing: humans are not made to live in water. It is clearly a dead man's spirit that she must go to honour on the shores where the earth comes to an end. Mutimbo has stretched out by her side. Such a thing would have been considered improper in their village, since both are married and they do not belong to the same family. The rules here in Bebayedi are different. There are not enough huts to keep men and women apart. And there is no reason to do so. Life adjusts to a new context. Eyabe hears a muted lament in the man's breathing, like a moaning that he represses in order to speak to her. His wound hurts. The foul smell from the poultice is not coming only from the remedy applied to the wound. It is also from an affliction that is unwilling to be defeated. She would like to take a closer look but it is dark and she is tired. What's more, when she hastily threw her things together before leaving, she did not take any medicinal plants, thinking that nature would provide. Looking back, it occurs to her that her surroundings changed in the course of the journey. She would not have known what herbs to gather. Maybe the residents of Bebayedi are still at the stage of discovery and experimentation. Maybe they have not yet found the plants that could heal Mutimbo. The woman yawns and shuts her eyes.

She is happy to fall asleep alongside a man from her clan, even though she is powerless to help him. She does not hear him explaining that the inhabitants of this new community have formed couples, knowing they will never see their own families again. They did not marry in the customary sense. People simply chose and accepted each other. One man for one woman. They recreated a space where life could thrive. Living is a duty. But he is too old for this. His heart will never throb for anyone but Eleke. Mutimbo has only one wife, which is unusual among Mulongo. Not being of the same social rank as his beloved, this restriction had been the condition of their union. It was never a problem for him.

Today, his sole desire is for his wife to know that his love for her is undiminished.

Eleke lives in every breath he takes, in every thought he thinks, in every vibration that emanates from him. When his eyes are shut, as they are now, he tries to travel to her, speak to her. The pain caused by his injury keeps him from doing so. Its intensity disturbs the energy he would like to direct towards his wife. The effort of concentrating exhausts him. He tried to carve a headrest to ensure the quality of his dreams. Unfortunately, he did not have the strength. And it would have had to be carved in bongongi but there is none in the area. There is mainly tanda, a small tree that thrives in marshes. Before coming here, he had never seen this species with roots that sink deep into the mud and rise like stilts over the water. Small fish and crustaceans cling to the roots. The children pick them off with their bare hands. He wishes there was bongongi here. Not only would it hasten the healing but also his spirit could travel unhindered to Eleke. In the place where she is at this moment, what does she receive from him? The man rests his head on a calabash.

In other circumstances, he might laugh at the idea of sleeping this way. Mutimbo does not find the situation funny. It is crucial to have proper dreams.

The dream is a reality. When sleep takes him, like now, Mutimbo's heart contracts. He does not like the nights he has been given since he came to Bebayedi. He sinks only halfway into the darkness, keeps an eye open in spite of himself, as shooting pains lacerate his groin, bring on fever. Every night unfolds the same way. When dawn comes, he no longer knows what he has dreamt. He feels like he has spent the night struggling not to scream. At times, he would like to perish, to leave all this behind. Death would release him from the sufferings of the flesh, he could deliver his message to Eleke, tell her that he is waiting for her on the other side.

*

What awakens Eyabe are not the first rays of dawn but the rattle coming from Mutimbo. She turns, leans over him. The man's eyes are open. His lips are moving but she hears no distinct words. The pregnant woman and the young mute boy are still asleep. She will have to climb down to seek help. She decides to inspect the wound first. The smell coming from it indicates that it needs cleansing. She barely touches the poultice and it falls off. The paste seems to have dried out, as if something had absorbed all the liquid. The flesh underneath is as black as pitch.

Eyabe recoils, certain that a worm, maybe more than one, is thriving in the wound. It smells of rotten meat. She draws near again, murmurs the first words that come to mind: she will be back soon, he must not worry. As she starts to move away, he grabs her wrist.

His hand is cold. He murmurs: *I do not have long to live. It is better this way. Sing to accompany me, as we do at home.* Eyabe̱ nods. She sits down, with Mutimbo's head on her lap and begins.

The Mulongo songs meant to give rhythm to the passage from one world to another are many. She did not think she would be choosing one before reaching the land of water, but she does not mind having to sing here. It is only right for the departing to be done before a witness, for the ancestors to be invoked. When it will be over, she will see to it that there is a vigil for Mutimbo, before burying him. The members of the Bebayedi community would not know how to sing the required songs. It would make no sense to teach them if they do not understand the words. She could however show the women the steps of the dance of the dead. She will also ask them to prepare a meal in which all will partake after the burial. Then, having nothing more to do in this place, she will continue on her journey in search of the land of water.

Eyabe̱ thinks over what Mutimbo told her about the shore he never saw, whose existence she never even suspected. He said that the course of the river called Kwa by the people of the marshes runs into a vaster expanse. She will walk along its bank to the ocean. The road may be long but now she knows which way to go. The fact that Mutimbo lived just long enough to impart this knowledge to her reinforces her determination. If the mission she undertook was not worthy, the spirits and the One and Only would not have let her to see him again. Thanks to him, she knows something about what happened to the twelve men who disappeared. It is important to stand where they last stood. At the end of the terrestrial world.

The woman would like to leave Bebayedi right there and then but it is not possible. She has been allowed to see Mutimbo again, to be there for his final moments. She cannot leave to others the responsibility of burying him, of watching over his entry into death. Once he has let out his last sigh, she will have to stay at least nine days and nights in this village. Preferring not to dwell on the obligations that will delay her departure, Eyabe raises her voice in song, heedless of the occupants of the hut. Softly she caresses Mutimbo's forehead. His eyes are closed now. The song soothes him, strengthens him. She is not singing one of the many chants that the Mulongo intone to accompany the dying on their journey. It is another unfamiliar tune that comes to Eyabe's mind, to confront this unprecedented situation.

Now she knows that the shadow that hovered over the hut of the women whose sons went missing is hovering over the world. The shadow drives communities to conflict, pushes people to flee their native lands. Once time will have gone by and moons will have followed on moons, who will retain the memory of all these displacements? In Bebayedi, yet-unborn generations will learn that their ancestors had to run away to save themselves from predators. They will learn why these huts are built over streams. They will be told: *Madness took hold of the world but some people refused to live in darkness. You are the descendants of the people who said no to the shadow.*

Eyabe lifts her eyes to the door. The sun is up, tranquil, nearly radiant. There is something strange about feeling so alone in spite of all, to seek the means of opening the doors for a soul on its journey to the other world. She cannot remember the words of the funerary chants. They are hidden somewhere in the back of her mind but she cannot retrieve them. Too many other things have gathered there. The woman shudders at the thought that old Mutimbo may be doomed to wander restlessly if she fails him. In her mind she asks Nyambe for forgiveness. She finds it impossible to concentrate. It is not even that she is thinking about her son. Her mind travels to the lands of the Mulongo clan where the women right at this moment are getting ready to go out to the field or to the water source. They have made sure the meal would be served, entrusting care of the household to their eldest girl.

Each woman will leave her family compound. Those who are going to the spring will meet in the village square, not far from the Council hut at its centre. Together they will walk to the source, will fall silent when they pass the dwelling of the women whose sons are missing. Eyabe wonders if her companions in misfortune are still living apart from the community. She bristles at the thought of this injustice, all the more since she now knows, based on Mutimbo's testimony, how impossible it is to entertain the slightest suspicion as to their responsibility. She thinks of Ebeise. Before the night they spent together in the communal hut, their exchanges had been limited to polite words. Common courtesies that did not always dissimulate an underlying mistrust. Yet, the midwife had become as dear to her as a mother. Eyabe caresses the amulet the elder gave her, hears once again the words she said when they left each other at the edge of the village: *Your journey will be long, my daughter. I do not know if you will find me here when you return. Do not worry about the men, I will take care of them...*

As Eyabe looks fixedly into the distance, on this peaceful day that seems not to be made for sorrow, a face appears in the opening. A woman steps into the hut, no doubt drawn by the singing. Eyabe does not move, she does not lower her eyes. The stranger approaches, sees Mutimbo's condition. The closed eyelids of the old man, his feeble breathing. He does not have long to live. Before nightfall the man will have breathed his last. The woman's cry frees Eyabe from her anxieties. She will not be alone to mourn the old man, to shed tears over him as is only proper, before laying his remains into the ground. It all happens very quickly. Soon other Bebayedi inhabitants are there. They carry Mutimbo outside. A raft is set up in the centre of the village to serve as a bier. It is covered with a mat.

In silence, the villagers step forward, surround the dying man. Eyabe does not understand the Bebayedi language. Only a few words have a familiar ring to them but clearly their meaning is different from what she thought. She has no time to wonder at the mystery of two languages that have obvious connections but remain alien to each other. The woman whose call has drawn the entire population is singing. Eyabe hears other voices of the women of the community respond in unison to the phrases punctuating the verses. She knows that Mutimbo will be carried to the other side in dignity. The tension in her shoulders eases. She cries. Her sobbing intensifies as her gratitude swells: Nyambe and the spirits have not abandoned her to her solitude. The Bebayedi, who have come into being out of pain, know better than anybody about the journey into death. They may not have left this earth but they have travelled from one world to another.

Men's voices join the women's. The mute young boy, seated on the ground near Eyabe, takes her hand. She does not know why but this simple gesture makes her weep even more. Two musical instruments accompany the chants. One has eight cords attached to a carved cane of sorts. The other has only one attached to an arc. Like the voices, they answer one another, carry words with them. What they say is accessible to anyone who knows how to listen. A thought crosses Eyabe's mind, she looks up at the hut that she just left to join the group on the village square. She is worried about the pregnant woman up there. She is immediately reassured at the sight of two young women standing at the door ready to assist her if need be. All is well. Mutimbo will not walk alone to the other side.

*

Heeding the chief's decision, the women whose sons went missing left the communal hut. The villagers submitted to three days and three nights of rituals to ward off evil. These women did too, although the Minister of Rites made sure, against the chief's better judgement, that they were placed apart. A few steps behind the other women of the community, they participated in the ceremony ahead of Mukano's departure. Peals of elimbi and ngomo tambours resounded for three days and three nights, quieting only to let the voices of the population ring out. Words circulated, incantatory, plaintive, hopeful. They danced to cast out bad energies. They danced to say things that words cannot express. Then the women who had been isolated were authorized to return to their family compounds, where they were not always met with a warm welcome. Each had been able to express herself during the gathering so that the bitterest of thoughts would not remain brewing in their hearts, but the atmosphere is still fraught.

Their co-wives look askance at them. The meals they prepare, when it is their turn to cook, are scorned. Their husbands always have something better to do when they are supposed to spend the night with them, apparently unconcerned that such neglect is an offence, for the Mulongo consider intercourse to be a conjugal obligation. The women whose sons went missing could bring the matter before the Council and have their husbands punished. They say nothing, looking back almost with regret at the time of their isolation. At least the situation was clear then. Alone in their huts, they feel apprehensive about having to go out to the fields. They know they can no longer expect, as they did not so long ago, to be supported in their efforts, to join with the others in sharing the crushed mbaa and the leaf sauce. They will be left to their solitude. No one will come help them when they need it.

Before leaving, Mukano vowed to bring back the boys. The mothers pray unrelentingly that it will be so. That all will see they committed no crime, they are not a gathering of witches who have come together to devour their own sons. Why would they? Even the women who did not hold their firstborn close to their hearts did not wish him harm. They never sought to hurt him. This child is a part of themselves, not necessarily the one they prefer, but they know the bond that unites them. The other women, those for whom the missing son is the most precious beloved of beings, cry without stop. The idea that they are suspected of taking their own son's lives cuts them to the quick. They do not have the strength to contain their feelings in front of the other village women. Ebusi is one of these women. More and more, she doubts the death of her son. Eyabe's child may have vanished into the land of water; hers is still on earth. Otherwise, she would feel it. Otherwise, she would have heard the words clearly that reached her muffled the day of the darkened dawn.

This morning, instead of heading to the spring where the women are soon to go, she directs her steps to Ebeise's hut. As she walks, she talks to herself, seems to see no one. She has not washed, not arranged her hair for several days. To what good? No one approaches her. Her children—she has two, aside from the eldest—treat her like a stranger. This is what is most unbearable. She had yearned so to see them again. Three weeks and a few days of absence sufficed for her to represent nothing in their eyes. Now she wants to ask the midwife for permission to return to the communal hut. There she will wait, the time it takes for her lost son to return. The hope of seeing him again is all she has left. As she walks, she rehearses what she will say to the midwife.

When she reaches Ebeise's compound, a torrential rain comes crashing down on the village. It is not the season for rain. She slows down, looks up at the sky, continues on her way. The downpour does not alter her resolve in any way. She is not afraid of the storm. It may even be a sign of approval from the spirits for the fury that is driving her. She walks on in the pouring rain, leaning slightly forward to withstand the power of the elements. Her lips move as she rehearses words that must not touch the ground, that must rise powerfully to be heard. Soon she will reach the compound where the midwife lives. In the courtyard, one of Ebeise's co-wives is scurrying back and forth to shelter the calabashes filled with various roots and vegetables from the rain. She is too busy to notice the newcomer who feels suddenly paralysed by timidity, hesitates to come in.

The wet ground makes her movements awkward. Never has she been here before. For each of her births, the midwife came to her. And the spiritual guide does not hold consultations in his family dwelling. He has a hut located outside his compound, a separate place that makes it possible for him to contain bad energies. The woman does not know in which hut she will find Ebeise. She stops for a moment in the middle of the courtyard, indifferent to the rain beating down on her head, flattening her hair. As she looks around, she mulls over the possibilities. In Mulongo country, things are precisely arranged. The dwelling of the first wife is always immediately to the right of the man's. The latter occupies an immutable position in relation to which the other huts are built. These thoughts guide Ebusi's steps.

A woman's voice interrupts her in midstride. She turns around, fixes her eyes upon the woman who presses a calabash full of vegetables against her chest. *You are Ebusi, are you not? Welcome. How can I help you?* The rain hammers the ground to the rhythm of the words addressed to her, as if two voices were singing at the top of their lungs two different tunes at the same time. Ebusi replies that she wants to speak with the midwife. Ebeise, it seems, has been gone for two days. She has not been back in the family courtyard since she left, which means that there is bad news. Ebusi claps her hands once, presents her open palms. By this gesture, she asks several questions: Where is Ebeise, and what situation is the woman referring to? Looking down at the leaves that are soaking up the rain, the woman gestures Ebusi to follow her into her hut.

The two women hurry to a dwelling. The cal-abash is placed in a corner, near the other recipients taken inside for shelter from the rain. Only then does Ebusi learn what is happening. *The mother of the household went to be with old Eleke who is ailing severely. She may not make it through the night . . . I do not think you will be able to see her in such circumstances.* Ebusi takes a hard look at the woman talking to her, sur-prised to see no animosity in her when the entire vil-lage has turned away from the women whose sons are missing. This does not change her feelings in the least. Going back to her family is out of the question. *Very well*, she says, nodding her head. *If Nyambe takes Eleke's spirit, it is unlikely I will be invited to the funeral. You will inform the midwife that I have gone back to the communal hut.*

*

By nightfall, Ebusi is seated in front of the dwelling where the ten women were living not long before. She feels almost at peace. Much more so than in the midst of her mistrustful family. She is not hungry, desires nothing. Her son must come back home. That is all. He must return, since she is waiting for him. Since she is truly waiting for him. Her thoughts cling to memory, to hope. This woman will live henceforth in her memories and hopes. Until her firstborn's return, she vows to continue to strengthen the bond between them. All her energy has to be directed to this end. Her mind must be entirely focused on the object of her love, so she can visualize him, reach him. She wants to summon him in her dreams, pierce the shadow that came to visit her at dawn a few days ago. If she can manage to bring back this dream, see the face of the person who spoke to her, he will return. This is what she thinks. In her self-imposed solitude, she invents a mystique of memory wherein feeling is an act, something more powerful than a force created by nature. What exists naturally only becomes good or bad in contact with a will. To this rule, there are only rare exceptions.

This willing is active in her now as never before. She looks at the earth, still damp from the rain, a deluge that nearly drowned misipo. On the soaked ground she sees the footprints of her little one. The baby is starting to crawl. He moves so quickly, you must keep an eye on him all the time. He will not sit still. The other women tease her. She must have eaten monkey when she was pregnant: that would explain why the little one will not stay put. She lets him go where he pleases without losing sight of him, but one day he escapes her attention. She holds back her tears, feverishly follows the tracks. The two small hands, the hollow left by a favoured knee. In fact, the only knee to touch the ground is the right one, the other leg he holds stretched out or slightly flexed as he forges ahead on all threes.

She finds him behind the hut, smearing mud over his face, laughing with glee. Ebusi smiles at the recollection. She starts singing the nursery rhyme she hummed when she took her child in her arms. She sings, pronounces the boy's name several times:

Mukudi. That is what he is called. Saying his name soothes her. Never for a moment did she think that occult forces could capture the vibration of this name. This belief, among the most rooted in her community, suddenly seems foolish to her. It is being named that makes what lives come into existence. By pronouncing her firstborn's name, she brings him back home, consolidates his presence there. This is what all the mothers who are waiting for their sons should do.

Ebusi concentrates, refuses to be distracted by anything. The noises that take hold of the night do not reach her. When a mournful cry rings down from the hill where the reigning family lives, the woman does not bat an eyelid. The clan has no need for her to cry over old Eleke. She does not feel that she is failing to fulfil her duties; her absence will not even be noticed. And little does she care. Let them come find her here, she will speak her mind. Soon she will go lie down on the one mat left in the hut, as if her return were expected. Ebusi feels she is where she belongs for the first time since the great fire. She forces herself not to raise her head, not to turn her gaze to the hill from where the cries are coming. It is hard to ignore them. They keep growing in intensity. The woman marshals all her inner strength to keep herself from being swept into the collective sadness. About her own pain, no one cares.

Eleke never had to experience the heart-rending pain of a son being taken from her. The woman lived a long life without anything of the sort happening.

She wedded the love of her life, married off her off-spring, saw the birth of her grandchildren, watched them grow up. The clan will carefully perform the rituals required to accompany the passing of her soul. Because of her rank and her status as healer, Eleke's body will be exhumed after a certain time. Her remains, bundled into a wooden reliquary covered in animal skin, will be preserved in a sanctuary. A guardian sculpture with four faces turned to the cardinal directions will watch over her rest. Her death will not be an end; she will remain strongly rooted within her clan. No reason then for Ebusi to be moved. This is how she sees things, as she watches the ash-coloured clouds gathering in the sky. Mbua, the rain, is approaching again. She rises, stretches for a moment, goes inside.

The drum call erupts at the same time as the thunder to announce the news. An oration begins, recalling, with every drum roll, who the deceased was, what the clan owes her. Already Ebusi hears no more. She speaks to her son, in a one-way conversation. She does not let the silence of his replies affect her. Her child will speak to her. He will be back.

*

No one dares approach, tell the midwife that it is not her place to perform these gestures. Chaos has taken hold in the community since the great fire. Nothing is done according to the rules. The deceased's sisters and daughters should be the ones to wash the body, apply ointments to the skin. In the hut where Eleke died, Ebeise takes up all the space. So the women of the family concentrate on other things, on arranging the places for the vigil, preparing the meal. When one of them makes a move to step inside the hut with the intention of choosing a mat to wrap around the body before burial, the midwife stops her: *Let it be. I will do it. This woman was more than my sister.*

The intruder nods her head, walks backward out of the room in a sign of deference. Ebeise does not belong to the lineage of Mulongo chiefs but everyone knows the ties that bound her to the woman who has just passed away. No one has the strength to oppose her. No one even wants to. Chief Mukano is absent. Mutango mysteriously vanished the day the shadow hovered over the communal hut. The spiritual guide is not there either. His son, Musima, will have no authority over the midwife, who is his mother.

When the rain stopped a little while before, one of Ebeise's co-wives, who had never climbed up this hill before, appeared before her. She had a message of utmost importance to deliver. As things were, all she could do was hold her tongue, take a seat on the stool that was shown to her in front of the hut. She is still waiting. She and the midwife have not exchanged a word. Any conversation seems compromised now. Ebeise is in deep mourning. She is not to be disturbed. Her co-wife will have to wait for it all to be over before telling her that one of the ten women, Ebusi, has taken it upon herself to go back to the isolated hut, without explaining the reasons for her act.

Busy with the care she is providing to her sole friend, the midwife is aware of presences around her. She knows someone has taken the trouble to come here to see her. She knows that the men of the Council, when they hear of the goings-on, will make their disapproval known. They have already reproached her for Eyabe's departure. *An extremely serious violation of our laws*, they bellowed. In the absence of Mukano, they did not dare sanction her. They did not know whether the chief had been informed, had given his consent. By the time they come here, she will have finished. There will be no offence to the children of Eleke who will take their rightful place at the ceremonies. This they understand, which is why they do not stand in her way. During all those days when it was clear to everyone that Nyambe was withdrawing the life force from the sick woman's body, the residents of the hillside saw that she only tolerated the presence of Ebeise. The midwife's deeds are just and faithful.

As she dips her fingers into a cup of njabi oil, the old woman recalls the last audible words uttered by her friend. Eleke said she could hear Mutimbo, distinctly this time. She smiled, adding that there was no need to worry about Eyabe: *Our daughter is safe and sound. She has not yet accomplished her task but all is well.* The midwife does not know what this means. The last words of the deceased remain a mystery to her. The Bwele were mentioned often but Eleke was too frail, she was already travelling. Ebeise feels overwhelmed by a profound weariness. She would like to withdraw to a quiet spot. Not see people any more. Not run from place to place to bring children into a world that is coming undone. *All is well*, Eleke said before closing her eyes. Maybe. In that case, they will see no inconvenience in her retreating for a while.

After the funeral, she will move into the hut left empty by the women whose sons went missing. There she will be able to rest, meditate, try to understand. Tears come to her eyes. Mundene, her husband, would have presided over the funeral ceremonies. Their son is full of good intentions but, like everyone else in the community, he is lost, does not know what to do. He lacks authority. Only the chief Mukano, who also exercises spiritual powers for the clan, could have adequately replaced the Minister of Rites. *All is well* ... She is not so sure but, with all her heart, she wants to trust in the dying woman's last words. When a soul is about to detach itself from the flesh, it sees, knows what others cannot perceive.

The first elimbi and ngomo drumrolls sound. Thunder explodes. Lightning briefly lights Eleke's face. She seems at peace, almost smiling. The midwife wraps the now cold body in a mat tied with solid straps, leaving only the head outside. During the vigil, the community will see the deceased's face, the serenity of her features. Heavy rain starts falling. For the second time today. Though it is not the season for it. Ebeise, now seated by the body, looks outside. She barely sees the people there, all those who will join her for the vigil to begin. She looks fixedly at the deluge. A rain like this will last several days.

She wonders if these waters, like the shadow darkening the dawn, affected only the clan's lands. Is it raining elsewhere too? If it is, then the community, which has not prepared for it, will find itself cut off for some time. They will have only themselves to rely on. Life will be hard for a population that has been deprived of its leader. Her withdrawal to the communal hut will not be understood. Her selfishness will be criticized. There will be talk of desertion. They will forget that she never failed them before in any way.

*

Mukano and his guards march to jedu. Since they left, they are doing their best to advance quickly, sleeping little, hardly stopping to eat, chewing nyai, the bitter white nut that combats fatigue. Was it on the day of Kwasi or Mukosi that they left the village to venture deep into the bush? Trained as these men are to remain vigilant, they have not been able to maintain their constant alertness and also keep track of the passing days. They are heading for a destination they will only recognize when they find their missing brothers. They would all like to be as determined as their chief, who has taken the head of the procession. As if he knew where he was going. He cuts branches to facilitate their passage. His gestures have the awkwardness of one who is unaccustomed to such endeavours. Their progress is slower than it should be.

The truth is they are not sure they are going in the right direction. The choice of paths was based on what the queen of the Bwele said. But what if she lied? So many questions are swirling in their minds. There is no objective reason to doubt Njanjo's words; some have misgivings nonetheless. Jedu is vague. Especially since they cannot get their bearings from the stars, which the thick foliage prevents them from seeing distinctly. They can rely only on the sun. It is critical for them to wake up a short time before dawn when the sun reappears under the name Etume, before becoming Ntindi, Esama, Enange ... Its fourth name, Enange, associated with its feminine incarnation, corresponds to the form it assumes at the end of the day.

The men do not utter a single word. They advance foot by weighty foot, scratching the nape of their neck and temples, left bare by their warrior hairdo. Their hairstyle, known as ngengu, is different from the other men in the clan and even from other warriors. They are the elite troops. The chief's personal guard. They are not allowed to say that they would have liked to explore the terrain before seeing Mukano venture out there. They are not authorized to complain, to say that their legs feel as heavy as njum branches, that they would like to rest for a moment. Have something to eat. Two guards, carrying the supplies, are bringing up the rear. They know the guards walking ahead will not look back at them but their loyalty prevents them from sneaking a piece of meat or some roasted seeds out of the sacks. What bothers the supply bearers the most right now is not so much to walk without knowing where they are going as to haul sacks of provisions when this is ordinarily the task of women.

For them, a mission for which men are forced to take on the rounded silhouette of women working the fields is doomed to failure. Never has such a thing happened in Mulongo memory. Of course, warriors have had to spend time in the heart of the bush in the past. They would hunt for food, as is fitting for men. This is not possible now, considering the circumstances. They are not to stop. Order of the chief. They must keep moving except when they halt to sleep a little, when the night shadows are too thick to continue. Last night they were ordered to defy even those shadows, to advance no matter what. They had already lost more than three weeks.

Mukano was eventually persuaded to listen to reason and agreed to a pause. But he did not close his eyes all night long. As they took turns on guard duty they saw him, seated, back against a tree, his mpondo over his shoulders, peering into the dark, perhaps perceiving signs in it. At times he was observed conversing with someone, an invisible presence. Then they thought that no, he was just chewing on roots or bark. By daybreak, they were on their way again, in silence. Mukano had a few glasses of bongongileaf juice, nothing more. Since they left the lands of their clan, he had eaten practically nothing. Such behaviour was worrisome. Out of respect and fondness for him, the men once again refrained from expressing their thoughts. But things could not go on like this: something would have to be done. There is no room for being downhearted when leading a mission such as this.

At the head of the march, the janea is the first to notice the change of terrain. The ground beneath his feet is waterlogged. Soon they are up to their calves in water. Plants unlike any they have ever seen rise before them on adventitious roots that reach deep down into the black mire. With his staff of authority, the chief tries in vain to drive away a swarm of insects buzzing in the stifling air. Dusk is coming. Dense heavy clouds are about to burst, to release a downpour that could hardly be welcome in a place like this. Mukano looks down at the strange shifting earth over which he must continue to advance. Even if they manage to get ahead of the pouring rain, will they ever step foot onto dry land again? Furrowing his brows, he tries to move.

The mud robs him of one of his mbondi, which disappears into the mire. He lifts his bared foot, looks at it as if for the first time. Or as if it belonged to someone else. The chief of the Mulongo thinks back on all the days that have gone by since the great fire. When was it that he failed? He must have done something wrong for Nyambe to abandon him. What was it? Should he have opposed the Council in its cowardice, had them look for the men who went missing as soon as the thing became known? Should he have revealed Mutango's crime, the incestuous rape the very night of the fire? Mukano sees every event; for a moment he even reproaches himself for having left his brother in the hands of the Bwele. Then he shakes his head. Criminals in Mulongo country, he thinks, are banished, left to the vengeance or leniency of the invisible. They are not put to death because human life is sacred. But they are driven out.

He simply cast a maleficent being out of the community. Then what? Should the women whose sons they are seeking have stayed in the communal hut? Should he have gone to see them when a cry was heard at the threshold of the night? Should he have waited for the return of the missing men to impose a ceremony on the clan? Before leaving the village, he took care to address the spirits. He himself has questioned the ngambi, though he did not receive a precise answer. He had had to content himself with these words from the oracle: *Son of Mulongo, nothing will be as before. The reign of Mwititi is upon us.* He had received no instructions. The decision was up to him and he made it in order to honour his rank. Evil, his father had taught him, exists only to be battled. Sometimes he added these words that Mukano had forgotten: *You have to fight without being certain that you yourself will see the day of triumph.* The Mulongo chief puts his naked foot down, lets loose a howl that the thunderclap quashes. It is raining.

One moon after Mutimbo was laid to rest, Eyabe set out on her way again. She stayed the month of mourning, for she was, in a sense, the only relative of the deceased. The time it took to learn the language of the Bebayedi, to make herself understood. The mute child, who had become attached to her, followed her now. She could not compel him to stay in Bebayedi. He walked by her side, his small hand in hers. Men from the community helped them go back up the river on a precarious raft. Every moment of the slow journey was torture. Hardly accustomed to water, she thought countless times she would fall into it, be lost for ever. Nyambe did not allow it. Their companions left them at the edge of their territory, where dry land regains its rights. When the time comes to return, she will have to wait several days for them to pass by. They seldom come here, out of fear they will encounter Coastlanders, reveal the existence of their village. The woman is ready. She will wait, this is what she tells the one to whom she speaks in a whisper. From Bebayedi, she will make her way back to the Mulongo village. The one who is listening bids her to recount her voyage. Nodding her head, she tells the story.

The strap of her bag was cutting into her forehead. At times, she would have liked to put it down, catch her breath. In those moments she talked to the child who did not answer her. It did not matter. She knew he was listening, that part of him understood what she said. They had walked at least two days, probably three, when she turned to face him, as she had already done in Bebayedi. Placing her hand on her chest, striking it several times, she repeated *Eyabe* until he nodded. *Eyabe*, he said, pointing his finger at her. The little boy's gravelly voice brought tears to her eyes. Misty-eyed, she put the palm of her hand on the child's torso. He replied, *Bana*. The woman laughed because the word means *children* in Mulongo language. She thought he was confusing the term with *muna*, which means *child*. That is what she had called him in Bebayedi. They proceeded on their way. He did not utter a word for a long time but he had become illuminated, open, reflecting various expressions. The woman did not ask more from him. When he will be ready to speak to her, he will do so.

As they walked, she continued to teach him the Mulongo language, naming the things in nature: leaves, wood, earth. The parts of the body. Actions: walking, eating, drinking, sleeping ... This gave her a sense of comfort. Sharing, transmitting. Making the world exist again for someone. At times, she would launch into long speeches on complicated subjects, such as Mulongo cosmogony and spirituality, which she wanted to recall. She needed to remember that she was not an isolated woman, lost in the immensity of misipo. She came from a people with a language, customs, a worldview, a history, a memory. She was the daughter of a human group that taught their children for generations that the divine manifested itself in all that lived.

One morning, she sensed they would soon reach an inhabited area. To drive away her apprehensions at the thought of meeting hostile people, Eyabe started to recite: *Nyambe is the creator of all things. By dividing his own force and scattering it, He brought the world into being. He is the all in which everything is gathered and united. Because humans cannot bear to see Him or even imagine Him, He chose to manifest Himself through secondary divinities called maloba. Every loba represents a part of the vital energy.* She paused, having forgotten the names of some of these entities, the names of their earthly manifestations. After a moment of silence, she went on to specify that the world was divided into four parts: *Dikoma, the dwelling of Nyambe; Sodibenga, where the maloba and the honourable dead live; Wase, where human beings live; Sisi, where the sun goes at night before it reappears at dawn, is the abode of ordinary ancestors and spirits.*

Eyabe was speaking mainly for herself. What she said was not as structured as usual. She lost herself in digressions, forgetting if the four elements were born from the marriage of Ebase and Posa, or if they were spawned by Ntindi and Ndanga-Dibala. Laughing nervously, she took note when she thought she heard a noise, slowing down and stopping. All of a sudden this enterprise seemed senseless to her. A woman had no business being on the road. If something happened to her, no one would know. The child pulled her hand, urging her forward. She looked at him not knowing what to do. So far they had been spared unfortunate encounters with ill-intentioned people or starving animals. Food had not been wanting, neither had places to take shelter at night, even if they had had at times to content themselves with sleeping under a tree. If she gave up on looking for the land of water, she would risk offending the invisible that had protected her.

Eyabe knew this. Yet she could no longer walk. She kept turning around, talking to herself: *And does the land of water, this ocean they spoke to me about, belong to Wase or to Sisi?* The elders made no mention of it. Suddenly fearful, she put her hands to her head, wondering why the midwife accepted to cover up her flight, why she had not held her back. In the village, she had always been criticized for her unfeminine ways. Had Ebeise wanted to get rid of an ill-behaved woman at a time when the community was struck by misfortune? Had she been banished without knowing it? Had she been sacrificed to the invisible in the hopes of restoring harmony to the village?

The one who said his name was Bana gingerly touched the pouch containing the jar of earth in it, which was banging against Eyabe's left side. The child's features at that moment betrayed a maturity and gravity beyond his years. The woman understood he had not followed her by chance. Maybe he had even been waiting for her there in Bebayedi. She fell silent. Now he was the one to speak: *Inyi*, he declared, *we are almost there.* She is not certain that he opened his mouth to utter these words but, having heard him, she would have liked to tell him that the name was not fitting for her since it is the name given to Nyambe in his feminine form. Inyi guards over the often-hidden connections uniting the elements of Creation. She is the feminine principle, the power that embodies the mystery of gestation, the knowledge of what is to come.

Eyabe would have liked to humbly take exception, refuse to become the supreme womb, so to speak. It was too late however to resist a destiny that she herself had chosen. Whether it was a banishment or not, she wanted to leave the lands of her clan. What drove her was more powerful than her fear. It would have been a wrong for her to remain deaf to the call of her firstborn. She had taken the responsibility of acting in the name of all the women whose sons had gone missing, all who had seen in their dream a shadow urging them to open the door.

The woman also recalled the rain that came pouring down just as Mutimbo's body was entrusted to the earth. The thunderstorm had been so dreadful she thought she would never be able to leave Bebayedi. The river Kwa, overflowing its banks, had invaded the land of the community, confining the people to their dwellings on stilts. She had to use all her powers of persuasion to convince the men to accompany her on the river when there was a lull. And when they left Bana and her, it started raining again. Oddly, the deluge seemed to be running behind them, coming down a few steps away, barely touching their heels. In the middle of this storm, lightning struck splitting a tree not far off right down the middle. That day they had walked from dawn to dusk, as quickly as they could and without stopping to eat or drink.

Then night had come. They had slipped into a makeshift hut, a crude shelter, probably for hunting. There, huddled against each other, they had waited several days for the rain to stop, afraid that the owner of the hut would appear at any time. He never showed up. *You are right*, she found herself saying, peering deep into Bana's eyes. *We are going to make it.* She did not wonder about how the boy had absorbed his lessons in the Mulongo language so quickly. She did not ask him if he meant to say Ina instead of Inyi: Ina being a feminine loba whose story she had told him, not the primal womb but the mother of all mothers. The time for questioning was over.

They did in fact make it, since here she is right this moment. She would never have thought it possible; she already felt fortunate to have been there to hear what Mutimbo had to say. When Bana and she crossed the threshold of this territory, they were surprised to discover the entry unguarded. She expected to find a town as big as Bekombo, the Bwele capital she had heard so much about, but there seemed to be nothing more than an ordinary village here. No sign of opulence or splendour comparable with what people who had visited Bwele country described. First she and Bana stopped to observe what was transpiring there. Then, cautiously taking a few steps forward, they saw that no one was paying attention to them. Busy as they were running to and fro, the inhabitants of the place simply did not see them. Most of the people were converging on the same spot. Eyabe thought the crowd would protect them, even though her hairdo and the scarifications on her bust would designate her as a foreigner. Silent in the middle of the throng, they would not be noticed. She would thus have time to come up with a plan. *And so we ran*, she explains, *like everyone else. That is how we arrived at the place where you found us.*

The people had gathered to attend the funeral of a notable, someone named Itaba, from what she understood. The men with hen feet were there, with solemn expressions, looking like they were suffering from the oppressive heat and humidity. Based on Mutimbo's description, it could only be them, even if he had never actually seen them. With those clothes of theirs, they did in fact have odd-looking legs. Other foreign dignitaries were there too, seated on stools reserved for their use. Over their heads were strange flowers in a shiny fabric that servants held aloft by their wood rods to keep the dignitaries in the shade. It was among these high-ranking guests, or, rather, alongside them, that she had recognized him.

She was covering her mouth with her hand to stifle a scream triggered by the spectacle before her eyes when a face had drawn her attention. *I wanted to keep myself from crying aloud when I saw the wives of the deceased plummeting to the bottom of the pit where the corpse was to be buried. That is when I saw Mutango.* So much weight had he lost that she almost did not recognize him. He was fanning a woman seated among the foreign dignitaries. The man to whom she is speaking says: *That is Princess Njole of the Bwele, Queen Njanjo's sister. From what I have heard, Mutango is now her servant. I do not know how this came to be.*

Eyabe tells him how Mutango vanished from the village the day that Mwititi hovered over the communal hut. The last time she saw him, before spotting him here, he was standing in front of the dwelling where the ten Mulongo women had been gathered. After that, she cannot say what happened, how the imposing notable, so feared in his village, could have become the docile servant of a Bwele princess. They will have to get to the bottom of the matter but that is not what is uppermost in her mind right now. Bana has fallen asleep, his head in the lap of the woman he calls Inyi. She looks at the man to whom she is talking. He knows what she wants to ask him, calmly forestalls her: *We will talk tomorrow. Try to sleep tonight.* Right now, he does not feel capable of telling his story. He thought it buried in his mind for good, with no possibility of it becoming part of the memory of his people.

The woman takes his hand. Will he at least tell her what this territory is? Is it the land of water that she set out to find? And who are these people with shaven heads? The man shrugs and replies simply: *I am like all these people. We are the ones that the waters did not bear away. The ones that the earth took everything from. We were robbed of the road that would have allowed us to go back home. We were deprived of our names. Unlike the people of Bebayedi that you have told me about, we did not manage to escape, to recreate our lives anew somewhere . . .* He falls silent, looks down at Bana who, mouth open, has surrendered to sleep on the lap of the mother he has chosen. The man looks long and hard at the child's face. A shudder runs through him when he speaks again: *As you see, this country belongs to Wase. But the earth ends here. Beyond, there is nothing but water. If the place you are seeking is the edge of our world, you have reached your destination. Mother . . . It is time for you to rest. And hold Bana tightly in your arms. We will talk tomorrow.* The woman is too exhausted to protest. She looks with gentle eyes at the one who has become a man in so little time.

He spreads a worn-out cloth on the ground. Eyabe lies down, draws Bana's frail body close and soon shuts her eyes. Recent events come whirling in her first sleep. She sees them from several angles as if her spirit were floating above the crowd. Details appear vividly. It is indeed Mutango there, holding a big dikube leaf in both hands, using it to fan a woman who does not even deign to look at him. It is he, head now shaven. His ritual scarifications indicating his rank are still there, but a metal bracelet fastened around his right ankle shows that he is no longer his own person. Eyabe knows this because some of the people in Bebayedi had one of these on their ankle until the blacksmith removed it for them. The man wore a simple dibato in barkcloth. His protective amulets were taken from him. When his arms grow weary, Princess Njolȩ casts a cold look at him that sets him going again. Clearly, he is scared of her. The woman terrifies him. How can that be? His mistress addresses a few words to him. He replies with gestures full of deference. At one point, she stabs his foot with an arrow, no doubt to prod him. His mouth opens as he struggles to hold back the cry rising from the pit of his stomach. Eyabȩ sees, in the middle of his teeth, the tiny piece that is left of his cut tongue. Shuddering, she averts her eyes.

Nearby is a woman surrounded by many attendants. Maybe it is Queen Njanjo. Her headdress hides her hair, temples and chin so that all you can see is her angular face. Like her sister, she looks fixedly ahead at the place where the rites are being performed. A high-ranking man addresses the crowd. He speaks of the deceased whose body, which was placed on a stool, is wrapped in a thick fabric. The orator is now naming the wives of the deceased, reciting their genealogy. They approach. The crowd cheers them, bursts into song. The women line up facing the hole dug for the corpse. A colossus waits to their right. After a few words from the orator, he steps forward, stands behind the first wife, picks her up, flings her to the bottom of the grave. His gesture is perfectly controlled. He will repeat it with each of the widows. None tries to flee. Some let out a cry that ceases when they hit the bottom.

One of the widows proves unwilling. Eyabe understands, in seeing Princess Njole get up, that it is a Bwele given in marriage to Itaba. Njole orders her to calm down, reminding her that to the Coastlanders wives are the property of their husbands. She must submit to the customs of her community through marriage. She will not be forgiven for behaving in a way that humiliates the people that engendered her. Eyabe does not understand Njole's language but can tell what is happening just by looking. When the archer princess draws the bow, inserts an arrow and aims, everyone in the crowd grasps the message. The recalcitrant widow falls on her knees. Cries. Implores. Njole utters one last warning. The rebellious wife stands up, casts a defiant look at the archer, slowly removes her headdress, her jewellery, her clothes. She then turns her unclothed back to Njole, thereby compelling all the dignitaries to look at her naked posterior. To the Mulongo, such a gesture is one of the worst possible insults. It calls forth a curse. Apparently, this is true here too. The rumbling that arises from the assembly is so powerful it seems to well up from the bowels of the earth.

Eyabe trembles. She wonders whether the children of the sacrificed widows are witnessing the scene. The sight of the women waiting their turn is unbearable to her. The seventh in line faints, collapsing into the hole without any assistance. Without a blink, the giant passes on to the next. It is at this moment that Eyabe covers her mouth with her hand to stifle a scream. It is at this moment that someone approaches her from behind, covers her shoulders with a colourful fabric, like some people in the crowd are wearing. Firmly holding her arms to prevent any abrupt movements, he gently draws her to him and whispers: *Mother, do not move. Do not turn around. Take the child with you and leave the crowd. I will be behind the buma.*

How long did it take her to know for sure he was speaking her language? Taking Bana by the hand, trembling she obeys, looks around for the buma, freezes when she sees it. It is the child, once again, who urges her forward. They walk around the huge tree trunk. The man is there. Alone. Head shaven. A metal bracelet around his right ankle. He does not embrace her, does not smile, does not ask what she is doing there, how she found her way to this place. With lifeless eyes, he stares at Bana. All three remain silent for a moment. The man speaks first, his eyes still riveted on the child: *Mother, allow me not to extend a welcome to you . . . Both of you, follow me. You are not safe here.* Eyabe does not witness the end of the burial. She has seen enough.

The songs of the population fill the air, joining with the frenzied beat of the drums. The woman and child move away without attracting attention. Eyabe stares at the back of their guide. She did not say a word to him, waiting to confirm that he is the person whom she believes she has recognized. Examining the bracelet around his ankle, she notices it does not seem to hamper his movement, barely slows his pace. Why then does he not run away? She saw when they entered the village that no one was guarding the entrance. At least not today. If he slipped away, no one would notice. This man may be a Bwele. After what Mutimbo told her, she is wary. Some Bwele can speak Mulongo. To prepare their attack at night, they must have observed the habits of their prey. Maybe this man saw her, maybe even several times, when she would go to the spring with the other women in the clan. Eyabe muses on all this but follows him nonetheless.

They cross most of the village, moving away from where the funeral is being held, away from any possibility of leaving the village too. If this is a trap, she will not get away. The woman tightens her grip on Bana's hand. They walk without approaching the huts, taking a path that deliberately skirts them. The deserted dwellings closely resemble Mulongo homes. All that is missing are the family totems planted in the ground by the doorways, the utensils used by the women to prepare the daily meal. A disabled old woman sits in front of one of the huts. Seeing them pass, she mutters something inaudible, sends spittle flying in their direction. The slimy substance hits the ground, just missing the passers-by. Eyabe looks away, clutches the hem of the fabric covering her shoulders. Soon, they reach a sector separated from the other constructions. Here are fewer houses, apparently hastily built. All except one building unlike any she has seen before, nearly as tall as a young buma, with white walls that seem to be cut in the rock. Eyabe stops. Something is troubling her.

This building frightens her. The only opening she can make out has bars on it. The woman did not know that such a thing could exist.

Her guide turns around. He gestures her to hurry. The place where he is leading them is very near these high walls. All around, dozens of people in this part of the village are not attending the funeral. All have a bracelet around their ankle, even the children. All have their heads shaven. For Eyabe, it resembles a community of people in mourning. She does not venture to think that it is their own disappearance that oppresses them. Every one of them was born from a woman. Each one was named, situated in a lineage. Each one had a place in a people. Each one was the depositary of a tradition. Are they still aware of this? How long have they been here? The emotion is too strong to spill out. Eyabe remains speechless. Mutimbo's words come back to her, she thinks she understands what is happening. It is obvious. Yet in her obstinacy to find the land of water to accomplish a sacred deed, she had not imagined finding herself faced with these figures. In a certain way, she had forgotten that the shadow had taken hold of the world.

The sound of water can be heard. She pictures a river, like the one that flows near Bebayedi. She recognizes the smell that has been bothering her since she arrived: it reeks of fish. She begins to gag. The man retraces his footsteps, faces her, says: *Mother, we must go. Follow me to the place where I stay. It is not very far.* This time she scrutinizes his face, lets her gaze slip down to his torso. The scarifications across his chest are those of a young Mulongo initiate. Those running across his temples tell her about his lineage. And this face. He looks so much like his mother . . . She was not mistaken. But why is he so cold? His attitude forbids outpourings. She would like to cry, hug him like the woman who brought him into the world would. Again he turns his back to her and all she can do is follow.

The woman hears the water, its presence stronger and stronger. Moans issue from the stony building that they pass before stepping into a hut as precarious as the others. Inside, there is nothing. Nothing but the bare ground, walls made of poorly assembled branches. This is where he lives. On his own. No one wants to share the space with him. He is feared because he does not speak. It suits him just fine. He does not wish for any company. *Son,* Eyabe says, *we will not be bothering you for long.* He lowers his head: *That is not what I meant. I cannot celebrate your arrival here but I will do all I can to make your stay tolerable.* Now that no one can see them will she explain how a woman could have found her way to the end of the world? He knows her reputation but the road is long from their country. Eyabe gratifies him with a sad smile: *I will tell you, of course. In the meantime, could you find something for us to eat? I left my sack in the shrubbery before entering the village. The boy has had nothing since . . .* The man interrupts her: *Mother, this one is a multitude. As you well know.*

These last words open the door for Eyabe to the second sleep. The deepest. As she sinks into it, what comes to her are not images of the past day but questions without answers. Where is the water she heard rippling? Who stays in the white building? Why do these people with shaven heads seem to accept their fate? Why is her host here and alone? What made him say that Bana was a multitude? Will she have the strength to make her way back home? What is happening in the village? Will the man want to come back with her?

Her night is restless. She struggles like an insect trapped in a spider's web. Many trials await her—this she knows. If her presence is discovered, they may shave her head. Put a metal band on her ankle. Then she will know what keeps the captives in this place. What prevents them from setting out on the road, on any road, in the hope of reclaiming their lives. The murmur of the water merges with her questions. Intermingling with cries from the stony building. Eyabe's rest is but a long quaking.

*

The ground is dry but life has not resumed as before in Mulongo land. Gathered for discussions in the meeting hut, the elders cannot reach an agreement. They concur on one thing only: Mukano remains the village chief but in his absence—and he has already been gone for quite some time—there must be a replacement. Who will hold this position in the interim? That is the issue. Since Mutango has disappeared, his fellow conspirators cannot propose his name. Of course, the chief has children but the oldest has not reached adulthood. He has not been circumcised. To entrust him with this responsibility would be wrong, even if the Council were to assist him. As for Mutango, who has many more offspring than his brother, he only sired girls. If he had been the clan's ruler, his successor would have had to be one of his grandsons once he had been initiated, had his foreskin removed. That would not be for some time. They are still sucking at their mothers' breasts.

The men have been sitting here since dawn. The sun will soon leave the sky to journey across the subterranean world. They are so oppressed by hunger that their stomachs cannot even rumble. And the nyai they are sharing during the meeting does nothing to alleviate their craving for food. As long as they have not found a solution, they are required to keep the discussion going until nightfall. This means they are not at all sure to find a hot meal waiting for them when they come home. The women are no longer willing to stay up too late, even if it is to feed their husbands. Everything has been coming undone since Mukano left. Disorder has taken hold.

Earlier in the day, one of the men came forward with a suggestion that provoked the ire of the others: *We would do well to hear what Ebeise has to say at a time like this. Can I send for her?* He was immediately cut down to size. The midwife chose to withdraw from village affairs. For once that she has made a reasonable decision, it is out of the question to demonstrate a lack of respect. The elder who made the recommendation prepares to take the floor again. He is not usually one to attract attention to himself at such meetings. He sits on the Council, though he would rather not, only because of his advanced age. Until now, he has always demonstrated unfailing loyalty to Mukano. It is not this situation, as exceptional as it may be, that will sway him from his course.

He clears his throat to indicate his desire to speak again. When all eyes are riveted on him, he takes the time to present the calabash containing the nyai, offering it with an unhurried gesture to each member in turn. He serves himself last, takes a bit of a nut, chews with difficulty since he no longer has all his teeth, sighs when he is finished, the slightest effort being an act of bravery at his age. The old man feels the tension rising. He knows the admonitions that his companions are straining to hold back: *Mulengu, what are you waiting for? Eh, Mulengu, it is not as if you had anything interesting to say.* Yes, he knows what they think. But very precise rules govern Mulongo communal life. Not only must the other sages listen to him with attention but also, if they do not share it, they must counter his opinion with well-founded arguments. Then, the Council members, one by one, will pronounce themselves for or against his suggestion. The old man's voice is clear when he begins:

We have reached an impasse. The father of Mukano and of . . . Mutango only had two sons. All the others are daughters. Some have given birth to males, that is true. However, all are married women subject to their husband's authority. If we were to go see one of them to announce that her son was to be chief, how would the father react? It is not easy to be obliged suddenly to obey one's progeny, even temporarily. And will the man who has had the staff of commandment confided to him temporarily be willing to give up the chief's stool once he has sat on it?

And how will we keep him from possessing the janea's wives? It will not be easy. I am telling you, my brothers, we do not have much of a choice if we want to preserve our clan. The community has been severely tested. The decision we will make will be unusual, to be sure. If it is to be understood by our population, it must have a certain logic to it. Which is why I think, given the situation, which none of us could have imagined, that there is only one solution: designating Mukano's oldest daughter as leader in the interim. Her husband will not take offence. When her father returns, she will give him back his place with no difficulty. And if he does not come back, power will be passed on to his oldest son when he is of age to exercise it. Cutting short the protests, the elder concludes: *Do not forget: this clan was founded by a woman. We are not acting, therefore, in contradiction with the history of our people.*

The silence that weighs on the Council is as crushing as a bongongi trunk. Most of the men seated there cannot see themselves pledging allegiance to a woman, requiring the men of the village to do so too. Even as an exceptional measure. The present-day generation of Mulongo did not experience the times of Queen Emene, who must have been inhabited by a male spirit. Otherwise, she could not have known such a destiny. The measures the elder is proposing are unacceptable. They would call into question the workings of their society as a whole. The sages are not in favour of it. They keep quiet, as they search for arguments more valid than their fear of losing their male prerogatives alone. Without consulting one another, they decide to put off discussion until the next day. It is getting late.

Old Mulengu claps his hands to adjourn the session. *Brothers,* he says, *we will resume tomorrow. It is not good for our people to know we are having difficulty resolving this problem. Let us now return to our families. But, I beg you, not a word to your wives. I advise you, also, not to spend the night with them.* The Council members nod in approval. Deep down, they resent him pressing them like this, pushing them into a corner. After all, it is only natural for them to want to maintain their privileges. If Mulengu cares so little, it is because he already has one foot in the grave. The honours and pleasures of this world do not mean much to him any more.

They leave the meeting as fast as their legs can carry them, banging their heads on the low ceiling, scraping their arms on the sides of the narrow door as they leave. From the look on their faces, you would think they had just been hit on the head with a pestle. A fire had been lit on the village square but they strain to adjust to the deepening darkness. Batting their eyelids, rubbing their eyes, stretching their stiff limbs, they linger around the Council hut, the time it takes to make out what is happening a few steps away. Engrossed in their discussion, the sounds in the village escaped their attention. Thus, they are unaware that the men responsible for guarding access to their territory have been knocked unconscious. They barely have time to realize that the silhouettes heading in their direction are Bwele hunters, led by a small man wearing animal skins. With a harsh wave of the hand, he commands his men to spread out in silence throughout the village. Some men stay by his side. He speaks in their language to the Mulongo sages: *We will not hurt you. Stay calm, everything will be all right.* His soldiers tie up the elders and gag them. *These men are worth nothing to us. We will leave them here.*

This time, the Bwele have no need to set the huts on fire. There are enough of them to carry out their long-laid plan. They have left nothing to chance. Instead of annexing Mulongo territory, taking their tribute in captives, Queen Njanjo was advised to opt for another solution. The recent rains were a determining factor in her decision. The unexpected deluge, lasting more than a week, convinced the Bwele sovereign that it would be absurd to subjugate a region that was inaccessible during rainy season. Unwilling to give up on putting this population to good use, she simply chose to displace them. This is the night that the Mulongo clan ceases to exist.

Unlike the Bwele, Mulongo warriors have not been trained to fight to the death. The most fearless are slaughtered. The others surrender, not knowing if theirs is the better fate. They capitulate because it is prohibited to deliberately expose oneself to death.

Cries ring out here and there. Insults are hurled, curses pronounced, pots of hot oil thrown in the face, pestles directed at private parts. The weapons they use to resist are laughable.

There is no way they can prevail tonight. Now they know where the great fire came from. Now they know that the shadow hovered over the hut of the women whose sons went missing to announce the disappearance of the known world. This they had not understood.

They all seek someone to blame. For some it is the ten women. The ones who are no longer waiting for their sons. They should never have been allowed to take their place in the community again. They are probably direct accomplices of the Bwele assailants. This explains the absence of Eyabe: she went to warn her partners in crime, tell them how to proceed. For others, Chief Mukano alone is responsible. Whatever the situation, a janea never abandons his people. He embodies those who came before him. Those whose stylized images are sculpted on the staff of authority. Those whose remains are preciously preserved in the sanctuary of reliquaries. A village deprived of its chief is like a chicken whose throat has just been cut: good for plucking and eviscerating. That is precisely what is happening.

Some of the elders think Mulengu's nonsensical ideas brought on the catastrophe. While they are being bound and gagged, before being thrown one on top of the other into the Council hut, they turn on him: *You see what happens when you try to up-end things!*

Do you even know what energies you have let loose? The old man withstands their wrathful looks, extends his arms so the Bwele can attach his wrists and replies: *It is just the opposite. We waited too long to put things back where they belong. We should have listened to Mukuno from the start. He understood that our sons had been stolen from us. If he had had our trust when he visited the Bwele queen, she would never have been able to deceive him.* Their assailants had not come to pay them a courtesy visit. Njanjo had sent them, after making sure the chief of the Mulongo clan was at a distance. What Mulengu was trying to do, in all modesty, was to preserve symbolically the figure of Mukano. To choose a replacement outside the lineage of the absent chief was to disavow him. *We had nothing to reproach him for, other than his probity. For once, take responsibility for your own deeds.* The gag they put on him stops him from saying anything more.

The Mulongo sages will die piled inside the Council hut. This they know. Already, the Bwele have left them, sure they will not be able to undo their bonds. They can no longer talk to or even look at one another. All they can do, willy-nilly, is listen to the cries, the sounds of fury for a time, then silence. The surrender of the survivors. They cannot help but imagine what they cannot see. Their people shackled, led in small groups in the bush. The Bwele evacuate the village, separate the inhabitants, prepare different convoys that they direct to specific locations in their territory. Reforming the Mulongo clan is out of the question. They would be running the risk of a rebellion. The men, especially the youngest, will be sent this very night to the coast. The women who have not-yet-born children will follow them at dawn. The formation of groups keeps the Bwele busy through part of the night. Now is not the time to rest.

Bwemba, the short man supervising operations, goes from place to place, issuing orders. Torches flare in the darkness. But they do not illuminate the place. Night has become more than a moment in time. It is duration, space, the colour of ages to come. Looking on as his hunters shackle a column of Mulongo men, the Bwele commander nods his head in silence, then gives a sudden jerk, as if startled by the sting of a bee: *Has anyone thought of destroying their sanctuaries? You,* he points to two soldiers, *go set fire to the reliquaries and to the chiefdom. Make sure nothing remains. Their Council hut will soon be but a tomb—no need to waste time on it.*

The two men break off from the group. With torches in hand, they reach the place where the reliquaries are kept, proceed without hesitation. It does not take long to reduce the soul and memory of the Mulongo people to ashes. They wait diligently to see the whole structure engulfed in flames before climbing the hill to where the homes of the clan's highest dignitaries stand. They are in no hurry. Their companions will not leave without them. There is no one here any more. Nothing to fear from the old men piled inside the Council hut who will draw their last breath soon enough. Gagged and bound hand and foot, they will only exhaust themselves struggling to break free.

As the Bwele sweep through the village, flaming branches in hand, their tall shadows flickering on the ground, they take no notice of the house built somewhat apart from the others at the end of the village. When the Mulongo were forced from their homes, this hut, nestled in an area covered with scrub on the edge of a field, did not attract attention. Yet two women are still there. The older one has imbibed a plant decoction that makes her sleep. She is so tired. She has not opened her eyes since she had the idea of taking the potion. She had not slept for several days before that. Several days of heart-rending sorrow. She is sleeping at last, a dreamless sleep. The other woman has withdrawn deep into herself, into the inmost depths of her being. Eyes shut, she squats at the back of the hut, rocks back and forth, recites words only she can hear: *Mukudi, answer me. Do you not hear me? Mukudi, she who brought you into the world is calling. MU kU Diiii . . . In the powerful name of Ina. In the name of Nyambe. Mu . . .* Since she moved into the hut, the woman has shut herself off from everything that lives outside. Seeing the midwife arrive, she did not address a word to her.

With her hands pressed firmly against her ears, she keeps herself cut off from the sound of the surrounding world. Thus, she did not hear the cries, the noise of fighting and running. Thus, she ignores the sound of two Bwele men passing by just now, setting fire to the chiefdom that was spared during the great fire. Ebusi's throat is dry but it makes no difference to her. Her mind is reaching out to her firstborn. She must speak to him, pronounce his name. If he is dead, she will know, she will feel it. You can sense such things. *Mukudi ooo A MUKUDI eee . . . I am waiting for you. I will not move from here. I am not afraid of anything. I will be here when you return. Mukudi, she who gave you to the light of day is calling. In the powerful name of Inyi . . .*

*

I know, says the man, *that such a thing is forbidden but what we were experiencing was already an overturning of all existing principles. All we knew was them and us. It made no sense. Yet there we were, walking at night on unlikely roads, heads shaven, wrists bound, naked like the children we had ceased to be, our necks bound between mwenge branches, so that all we could do was look straight ahead at the nape of the person walking ahead of us in the column. We spent so much time struggling to keep step that soon it became the only aim. During stops, we could think of other things. Have other things in mind aside from the fear of not keeping up, of tripping, bringing our brothers down in our fall. Naively, we must have thought that keeping up the pace under such conditions was a demonstration of strength. Proof that it was not all over. We would give them back their due when the time came. Very soon we realized this was not to be.*

Our enemies were many, well armed, constantly on our backs. Impossible to speak to each other. We could not even make a sign without arousing suspicion. So I stopped eating. I did not dare invite death out loud but I fervently wished for it. When, on the third or fourth day, I cannot recall any more, our Uncle Mutimbo stopped walking, a Bwele warrior drove an arrow into his groin. He collapsed. We left him behind. Before I heard from you what became of him, I pictured hyenas feasting on his corpse. This image haunted me for a long time. We could not even turn around to see him once more. I am not saying anything about paying him the respect due to a man, but a mere look. These people stole everything from us. Everything. On the way, we heard some of them speaking candidly. We understood their language a little since we were used to the notables of our clan hosting Bwele merchants, but most of what they said eluded us. We had just reached adulthood, had never before left our land. I suspected what you have now confirmed, that our uncle Mutimbo resisted because he had overheard something. He did not have the time to tell us.

As the days went by, I grew weaker and weaker. The column slowed down because of me but did not stop. Death categorically turned down my petition. It let me reach the end of the long road with my brothers. The Bwele turned us over to the people here, after heated discussions. We were examined, counted. There must have been twelve of us—so one was missing. In addition, I was too weak, our Uncle Mundene too old. The Bwele wanted to be paid all that was promised to them, arguing that they took all the risks. Their protests triggered an outburst of laughter from the Coastlanders. Apparently, they were the ones who had recruited Queen Njanjo's hunters for the raid to seek captives. Old Mundene explained these things to us once they left us alone.

It was the first time since our abduction that we found ourselves alone. It was too late to be of any use to us. We were held in the white building you saw earlier. Imprisoned there, we dragged our feet with metal shackles on our ankles. If we had wanted to escape, we would not have been able to. First, we had these fetters. And then we did not know where to go to return home safely. It would not have been hard for our jailers to capture us again. They kept close. Not the Bwele any more, whose language we understood. But the people from here, the Isedu, also called Coastlanders.

You were surprised to see how easy it is to enter this territory. It is simply because they have no need for guards. Their cruelty is rampart enough. Human life is not sacred to them as it is to us. For them, for the Bwele too, war is a ritual, a macabre ceremony. You saw the funeral rites for their dignitaries. It seems that funerals for princes are held in secret. Not only women but also several notables are thrown into the pit on such occasions. It is considered an honour. They believe, like us, that death is but a voyage, even if no one wishes to embark on it too soon . . .

One day, they took us out of the prison for a walk and some fresh air. They would use such occasions to dump water over our bodies. This time they brought us outside but not to stretch our legs. They took us to an open area near the ocean. Men with hen feet examined us in a way that common decency prevents me from relating. Then they turned away, began negotiating with Prince Ibankoro, sovereign of the coast. We did not understand their exchanges but knew they were about us. Now I know that the foreigners who came across the waters from pongo complained they had had to wait too long for this delivery. They were behind schedule, demanded to take us that very night, refusing to provide some of the merchandise that was expected in return. We were not all choice catches. Mund*ene* was too old. They did not know if I would live. And a man was missing, since he had been abandoned to scavengers.

In the end, they took us back to the white building. The ocean roared as it threw itself on the sand, with an outpouring of foam that we feared would touch our feet. We leapt on the shore. Never had we imagined such a vast expanse of water. From our prison, we saw it rearing and prancing through a crack. I looked only once. The others took turns peering through the tiny opening, trying to make sense of this moving expanse. Your son, Mukate, was one of the most insistent. The ocean became an obsession to him from the time he caught sight of the 'ship', the vessel of the men with hen feet. After a while, he became convinced that the ocean was a passageway to the subterranean world that the sun crosses at night. He thought that if the foreigners with hen feet came to earth by way of the ocean they must be spirits, inhabitants of the world below. I kept silent when he talked about his vision of things. For me, he was far from the truth—I thought it was pointless to probe the ship in order to fathom the world below. We had already fallen into it.

Eyab*e* sat up with a jolt. The man just uttered her son's name for the very first time. Until now, he did not name the young men of his age group, as if pronouncing their names would expose them to danger. She pays close attention to his words, holds herself back from interrupting him, hoping he will come to the part of the story she is waiting to hear. She needs to know why a call came to her from the land of water. What happened exactly? Where are the other sons of the clan? Why was he the only one to stay in this strange country. At the end of a very restless night, she found him sitting in front of the door to the hut, looking in the direction of mbenge, from where the rippling of water could be heard. He looked as if he were conversing wordlessly with this space that she saw as the brink of the shadowy part of the universe.

Eyabe had turned around to where Bana was sleeping, fists clenched, in a state of surrender she had never seen him in before. The idea that he might not wake again crossed her mind, prompting her to approach him in a movement of panic. That is when the man's voice was heard: *Have no fear, Mother. They will not leave without saying goodbye. Let them rest.* She did not ask for an explanation, though the question was burning on her lips, she joined him, sat by his side, looking off in the same direction. The water was out of sight, but you could tell it was nearby. Seeming to know no rest, it went from a murmur to a roar, rumbling, blowing, sighing, sounding, in the middle of the night, like a chorus of suffering souls. Without seeing it, you were aware of its influence on everything living in the vicinity. Even the air here is different, permeated as it is with smells unfamiliar to the Mulongo woman whose clan once lived deep in the heart of the bush.

First, the man had begun to talk of the people who lived in this last region of the world. They were called Isedu. They presented themselves as having been brought into the world by the water that they revered. In reality, it was a dispute with their Bwele brothers that drove them, many generations back, to the confines of the realm of the living. While making their way to the coast, they attacked the communities that lived in the bush between Bwele country and the place that was to become their territory. *These peaceable populations had to pledge allegiance to escape with their lives . . . If you had taken the same roads we took to come here, you would have travelled through the area where some of these people still live.* We thought the Bwele and the Coastlanders were simply allies but they descend from a common ancestor, Iwiye̲, who had two sons. When they reached manhood, the father demanded that each find a land for himself, become the founder there of a clan.

The elder, called Bwele, conquered a vast territory, including the land inherited from their ancestor. The younger, Isedu, complaining that the worst areas had been left to him, confronted his brother in battle and lost. That is why they had to retreat to the coastland. Not so long ago, his descendants were still less powerful than the Bwele. Yet they were driven by an ill-concealed desire for revenge. The Bwele sovereigns concluded agreements, in different periods, with their vindictive brothers to avoid incessant conflict, to contain their bitterness, prevent them from causing harm.

Then, the foreigners, who came across the waters from pongo, appeared. Ikuna, the grandfather of Ibankoro, was ruler at the time. His son, Ipao, succeeded him later. The Coastlanders quickly realized the benefits they could draw from relations with the men with hen feet. The latter gave them remarkable merchandise in exchange for oil and elephant teeth or tusks. They were the first to wear fabric woven by the foreigners. These fabrics with printed patterns became very fashionable among the Isedu. Then their princes acquired weapons that spit fire, make a thundering sound. When their trading partners began demanding people in exchange for these weapons, the Coastlanders first turned over some of their vassals or individuals who had seriously transgressed the clan's laws. In exchange, they only accepted these famous tools of combat.

As time went by, the demand for human beings grew. There were not enough vassals and troublemakers in Isedu land to satisfy the men with hen feet. The Coastlander princes, eager to equip their elite battalions with these new weapons, did not hesitate to take prisoners from the Bwele. Operating at night, they mainly raided villages closest to their territory. It took a while before the Bwele kings, residing in the capital city of Bekombo much farther south, learnt about what was going on. A council was held with dignitaries from both communities. The Coastlanders were called to order. They had no idea what the men with hen feet did with the people they brought them. For this reason they were careful not to hand over people from their own ranks. They were told that the captives would go work for the foreigners but they had no way of verifying this.

Once, the men with hen feet had taken hostages from the Isedu community to pressure them to deliver the human merchandise in exchange for which they had already provided what was expected of them, and even more. In keeping with local custom upon arrival on Isedu territory, and as dues for the right to anchor in local waters, they brought fabric, clothing, jewellery, various utensils, foodstuffs and drinks—catering in this way to the tastes of the princes and their entourage, which they were beginning to know. In good faith, they had then handed over metals and weapons, the only merchandise accepted in exchange for captives. Since the captives had not been delivered to them as promised, they had helped themselves to people from the Isedu population.

The hostages had been given back after several months. Upon their return, they had recounted their adventures in the lands along the shores of the ocean to which the men with hen feet travelled to fill the belly of their ship. They had told of the merciless battles of some populations that refused to trade with the foreigners from pongo, no matter what the cost. When this was the case, the latter forcefully captured the obstinate, shackling even the people of high rank. These stories had convinced the Coastlanders of the need to ensure peaceful relations with the men who had come across the waters from pongo. At any rate, they had no intention of acting otherwise. To the

Bwele, they had claimed without flinching that they had no other choice than to satisfy their trade partners, to do all they could to find human merchandise for them. Naturally they had no desire to travel far and wide over misipo to achieve their purpose. All the more, since they could obtain what they wanted from their closest neighbours, people whose ways they knew perfectly well and for good reason.

Hearing these words, the Bwele vigorously objected. Relations with their Isedu brothers had been peaceful enough until then. Why destroy it all? Why had they not sent emissaries to their brothers to discuss their difficulties and find solutions together? Why treat their brothers like enemies? The time of ancestral quarrelling when the sons of Iwiyẹ fought to establish their respective territories was long gone. Now they could speak to each other. And so they made a pact. The Isedu refused to lose the benefits of trade with the foreigners. For the Bwele, it was out of the question that they be continually attacked, even if the injured parties were only tribes subjugated by the clan's founder, always the object of disdain to those who could claim unquestionable Bwele ancestry. *They are ours*, they maintained. *We added their gods, languages and culinary habits to our own. They are part of us now.*

This declaration of fraternity towards the conquered peoples meant one thing only: demanding a tribute from these communities was the prerogative of Bwele sovereigns alone. They exercised this privilege every time they needed people—which was often—to work in the fields or serve in the homes of dignitaries. These workers were well treated. They did not cut their ears as they did to the people they conquered. Certain activities, such as forging or weaving, were inaccessible to them but their participation in the general interests of the group was recognized. If they were now going to be deprived of these servants, they would have to be compensated in one way or another. To conclude, Queen Njanjo and her entourage saw no reason why they should be denied access to the goods brought across the ocean from pongo, merchandise that lent prestige to the Coastlanders.

The Bwele proposed to officiate as providers of prisoners. They would take charge of the capture; in exchange for their services they would receive the goods that interested them. The Isedu agreed to this, insisting however that the fire-spitting weapons and the powder that fed them be exclusively their reserve. The prowess of the Bwele as warriors was well known. They had perfected different sorts of knives that they handled with uncommon dexterity. They could also count on their archers, equipped with keen sight and poisoned arrows, to leave no chance to the enemy. But, with their new weaponry, the Coastlanders thought they would soon have the competitive edge. That is how they had managed to defy their brothers, force them to accept an agreement on their terms. Relations with the foreigners with hen feet had become so sustained that the latter decided it would be useful to put up a building for the detention of captives. It was said that soon the firstborn sons of the great Isedu families would be sent to the land of the men with hen feet. There they would receive instruction, in view of consolidating their dominant position. The Isedu would then be able to exact revenge on their brothers, seize the territory they coveted since the birth of the two clans.

Already, the foreigners who had come across the waters from pongo were spending more and more time among the Coastlanders who were taking them into the bush. Until then, they had only stepped foot on land for their transactions. Now some of them were invited into the homes of noble families, were offered women, were learning to speak the local language, while words from their language had enriched the Isedu tongue, notably when it came to naming the goods they brought with them in their vessels. To avoid being overly dependent on their enemy brothers, this generation of Isedu took risks. When trading in vassals or in transgressors did not suffice, they began travelling up the coast in pirogues to locate populations unknown before the return of the hostages who mentioned them in their reports.

Unlike the men with hen feet, they did not venture to attack them on their land. Instead they laid traps on the water. These perilous operations could not succeed without the use of their new weapons. They also needed to be carried out meticulously and by the very best oarsmen, the most accurate archers, the most skilled marksmen. It was said that soon the Isedu would extend their prospecting along the river flowing on the edge of their territory or on its other bank. This river flows into the ocean. The man could not be sure, but it could very well be the same waterway that brought Eyabe from Bebayedi. One could only hope that the distance and the swamp would continue to protect this territory.

Capturing operations were in full swing. The Mulongo, like others, had found themselves implicated in something that went beyond them. The night of the great fire, when the Bwele had taken captive twelve men from this community, the Mulongo were far from suspecting that their misadventure was but one among so many other intricate incidents punctuating a complex history. How many men, women and children from how many peoples were wrenched in the same way from their families, catapulted onto often-unfamiliar roads to end up here at the very edge of Wase? The situation was easy to understand: Ibankoro, the current Isedu prince, had decided to go even farther than his forerunners in the production and commerce of captives. Before his father's death, he had already convinced the elders that some of the demands formulated by the men with hen feet were justified. He was the one to whom the foreigners were indebted for being allowed to build the structure in white stone. It served as a warehouse, not only for supplies for their ships but also to hold the abducted.

It was said that his Highness Ibankoro, dazzled by the majesty of the building, had asked his friends with hen feet to build a dwelling worthy of his rank on the same model. This prince was among the Isedu dignitaries who had been beguiled by all that the foreigners with hen feet had brought them. The women of this cast spent their time admiring themselves in objects that showed them their own reflection. Many no longer ventured outside without fans in the shape of huge flowers with petals cut in a shiny material. Their servants, gripping the wooden handles, held the artificial flowers over these illustrious figures to protect them from the heat of the sun. Dismissing the mabato in fibre or bark as beneath them, the high-ranking women wore only printed fabrics that the foreigners with hen feet were said to have made solely for the pleasure of the Isedu dignitaries. The foreigners themselves did not wear these colourful fabrics.

Ibankoro did not step foot outside his family compound without a head-covering embroidered with luminescent threads and a string of bright red beads hanging from his right ear. Several strands of necklace jangled around his neck to the rhythm of his steps, signalling his presence even before he showed himself. He had a particular fondness for the finery given to the notables by the men with hen feet, but that was not all he liked. Aside from the fire-spitting weapon that never left his side—and he delighted in sounding two shots at any pretext—he had a singular taste for the alcohols that were brought across the waters from pongo. All these new products endowed Isedu society with a prestige that could supplant the refinement of the Bwele art of living. Needless to say, the Isedu were not about to give up a commerce that would allow them one day soon to dominate the communities descended from the Iwiye ancestor.

Only after this long account did the man turn to telling the story of the events that took place the night of the great fire. Now, he has stopped speaking. Eyabe does not know how to urge him to continue. Timidly she asks: *How did you learn about all this? I mean, the history of these people?* He shrugs: *Mother, it would take too long to tell you. Like other people with shaven heads, I was in the service of an Isedu nobleman for a while. He was not satisfied with me. I was brought back here—that is all I can say. More time has passed than you imagine since my brothers and I have been abducted.* The man falls silent again, stares out at the horizon, the invisible ocean. Eyabe contrives a digression, hoping to reach him, get him talking again. He is so cold, seemingly absent from his own body at times, bereft of strength. Perhaps he needs to recall the village, the one he left, to find his footing again in life.

The woman thinks that the memory of his mother will give him back the will, the ability to fight his melancholy. So she says: *Ebusi's thoughts are turned to you. Will you come back with me? Think how happy she would be.* The man looks at her wide-eyed; in his eyes she sees a rush of emotions but she cannot identify a single one. *Do not pronounce that name again in my presence,* he rasps. *I will not be going with you. I cannot live among you any more. It does not matter what I endure here.* Eyabe does not know what to say. *Mukudi,* she starts feebly, groping for words. But he does not give her the chance. *Do not call me that any more. That was my name in another world. In this one, I am neither a son nor a brother. Solitude is my abode and my only horizon.*

Like the other men with shaven heads, hanging around waiting for their fate to be sealed, he considers that he has no past any more. He thanks the maloba for having allowed him to see Eyabe again, but this opportunity was given to him for one reason alone: to relate the events that took place the night of the great fire and the following days, before falling definitively silent. His is a world of never-ending night to which he has grown accustomed. To him Eyabe and Bana are like stars in the heart of darkness, though he does not show them the gratitude he feels to have them there by his side for a while. But they will have to leave. And he will remain here so that someone will remember. Eyabe cannot conceal her impatience any more. Yet her intuition tells her not to ask him straight out, *What can you tell me of Mukate, my firstborn?* Instead she simply says: *I have come to accomplish a sacred deed. When will we go to the ocean?*

Mukudi shrugs. The men with shaven heads do not have the right to approach the water. It is forbidden because many before them were drawn by some unknown force into its depths. They are free to move around the perimeter of the village where they live. Anywhere beyond they must be accompanied. *I should not even have gone to the square to watch Itaba's funeral.* He had taken advantage of the fact that everyone was forced to attend the event to slip out of the sector reserved for captives. No one paid attention to him. Going to the seashore would be a different matter altogether. Coastlander notables built their homes there to stay in proximity to the spirits of the water. And that is where 'the ship' is to be found, as the huge craft of the men with hen feet is called. Some forty-odd foreigners reside in that area, that is where the trading takes place between them and the Coastlander princes. Impossible to go there. They would be laying themselves open to unmentionable perils.

Eyabe nods. *I hear you, son. But I have not come all this way for nothing. There*, she adds pointing to the ramshackle quarters where he spends his joyless days, *I have something to pour into the ocean. The maloba let me hear Mukate's voice. I have to do this to free him, permit him to make his way to the other world.* She gazes into the man's face, hoping these words will move him to tell her more. If he is afraid of breaking the news to her of her firstborn's death, she wants him to know that this she has already understood. Only the details are missing. The elements that will enable her find out what took place. She must know, precisely, the fate of the Mulongo men torn from their people. In such matters, nothing is worse than ignorance. The women whose sons went missing must have knowledge of the truth.

The woman declares that it is imperative for her to go to the shores where the earth comes to an end if she wants to go back to the village with answers. So that the Mulongo people will stop letting their imagination carry them too far. So that confused thinking does not become a new way of life in Mulongo country. So that the women whose sons went missing will be cleared of all suspicion, fully rehabilitated. As long as doubt persists, harmony will be compromised. The man shuts out her words. He does not want to speak any more, has no intention of going with her to the shore. *Give me directions, I will go without you,* she says simply. *And I will not tell Ebusi that I saw you, if you ask me not to. Your mother will not understand your decision to stay here.* He nods in agreement. *We will have to shave your head,* he murmurs. *Set out at night, so as not to attract attention.* He hesitates, then concludes: *I do not know that I can summon the strength in me to approach the ocean.* Bana's voice interrupts their conversation. He has just woken up. With a smile on his lips, the child peers into Mukudi eyes: *I will go with Inyi.*

*

The matriarch rubs her eyelids, rolls over, reluctant to open her eyes. She tries to fall back asleep but the effects of the potion have worn off. Her efforts are in vain. Reluctantly, she sits up on her mat, scans the room with a confused look. Ebusi is asleep in a corner of the hut, squatting, with her hands over her ears. When her body begins to slump, she straightens up, reflexively, continues to mumble in her slumber a litany of pleas to her missing son. Ebeise watches for a moment, wondering if she should urge her to lie down. This woman is doing exactly the opposite of what she should if she wants to converse with the invisible. Concentration is essential, to be sure. But it is crucial too to banish febrility. Then one must penetrate into the night, be receptive to rest, for it is conducive to dreaming.

If Ebusi wants to talk to her firstborn, if she wants to see him, she must put herself into a dream state. The elder will explain this to her when the time comes. Right now she does not want to communicate with anyone. She gets up, stretches, takes a few steps outside. Out of curiosity, she would like to know what day it is, even though, having retired from the world, it is of no real importance. Judging from the dose of sedative plants she used for the potion, she knows she has slept at least two days. She did not dream. It was her intention not to. Dream activity sometimes stirs up questions and troubles. She has had her fill of tribulations.

Hands on her hips, standing in front of the hut, she scans the horizon. The sun is high in the sky. Yet the village is sunk in nocturnal silence. None of the usual sounds of children playing. Their mothers are also silent when they should be scolding them at this hour, swearing they will be punished if they do not behave. And what about the men? Where is the sound of their work songs as they rebuild the village? Something is not right. For an instant, the woman wonders whether she is still sleeping. She thought she had done her best not to dream but her mind must be altogether too restless.

It must be a vision, of the type that comes in the third sleep, that takes you travelling to other dimensions. Maybe she would be better off lying down again to put an end to this journey that she has no desire to take? As she is about to do so, something attracts her attention. Ten to twelve steps away, a hen is pecking furiously at what looks like a human head. Her sharp eye has never led her astray. The midwife is fairly sure of what she sees. As she watches its beak dig into the sockets, sink into the nostrils, Ebeise cannot help but think that, dream or not, she has to take a closer look.

The Mulongo midwife approaches the scene with slow steps, railing against a life that refuses to give her any peace. She complains that dreams, even dreams, are not what they used to be. In a dream worthy of the name she would not have to walk like she is doing now. All she would have to do is will herself there, right by her son Musima's hut, to be there instantly. She advances grumbling, with a tingling feeling on the soles of her feet; that sensation too she would happily do without, after all, she is dreaming. A very unpleasant smell is hanging in the air, something she cannot identify. It is not exactly the smell of rotting but it is close to it. Ebeise is surprised to hear nothing while at the same time sensing things with such intensity, in the air, beneath her feet. Never before has she dreamt this way. She will have to be more careful next time when making the sedative decoction. She did not measure all its effects.

Her steps bring her close to the hen. It picks up its head, looks at her, goes back to what it was doing. At a steady rhythm, its beak strikes the head which rolls this way, then that. Ebeise stops. This bird is not what it seems; that is obvious. What she sees can only be a message. In Mundene's absence, how is she to interpret it? It would be pointless to turn to Musima for help; he lacks the calibre needed to enlighten her. She wonders. If her dream is confronting her with such a situation, it means she must act. It would be absurd, after having been led here, for her to do nothing more than take notice, then turn on her heels. Without much conviction, the woman lifts her arms, waves them in front of the hen that should understand that it is being chased away, that it is not fitting for it to scrape the skin off a human head, to tear off pieces of flesh. The midwife's gestures elicit no reaction.

Ebeise must take one more step, bend down to rescue the bodiless head. She does so grumbling. Destiny is unfair. Why is it that some people know no rest, not even in their sleep. She swears that when death will take her she will not reincarnate. No matter how the community feels about it, she will go sit among the blessed whose only obligation is to appear from time to time to assist the living. And these appearances she will make only sparingly—this she promises herself. Grabbing the head, its skin torn, its sockets empty, she sends her foot flying at the hen to drive it back. Instead, it plunges its beak into her calf, latching onto it so tightly it almost seems to have a jaw. Ebeise spins around as fast as she can, but the hen hangs on, will not let go. Looking down at her leg, holding her head in both hands, she shakes, hops, stamps her foot, teeth clenched, gasping for breath, eyes red with anger and pain, determined not to cry out, because one must see things as they are: it is only a hen.

The midwife would like to wring its neck, show it who is in charge. A spirit that chooses to live in the body of a hen, that has found no better way to manifest itself will not get the better of her. She must free up her hands if she is going to defend herself as she must. The woman gets ready to apologize to this head that did not deserve to be dropped like this. In a roar of horror, she sees it roll to the ground. No need for her to pick it up again for a second look. In this moment when absurdity competes with horror, Ebeise knows with certainty that it is the head of Musima, her firstborn, that has just slipped from her hands. Since the worst nightmares come to an end, usually abrupt, now is when she should be opening her eyes, wondering what all this could possibly mean. She should be waking up in the hut by Ebusi's side, promptly burning bark to chase away the anxiety. Trying to understand.

She is not spared hand-to-hand combat with the hen. Trembling with rage, eyes filled with tears, she manages to hurl it far away. Blood trickles down her calf, but she pays it no heed. She looks around for the head. It collided against the foot of a tree, is now covered in earth. The old woman takes a deep breath. The odour she could not name fills her lungs, leaving no doubt. It is the smell of death and it is not an omen. Did she commit an offence in deciding to withdraw? Must she pay such a high price for it? Ebeise tries to put some order into her thoughts. Even the horrid Mutango would not have killed her son like this. And aside from him, no one would think of doing so. The Mulongo are little inclined to shed blood. Before killing an animal for food, they ask its forgiveness. And ever since Mukano became the janea, sacrifices have become rare. Something very serious happened while she was sleeping. Serious enough for her to put an immediate end to her retreat, ask for a hearing with the Council. How is it possible that she hears no cries from Musima's widows? Where are the inhabitants of the village when a hen is feasting on the remains of her child? Ebeise has always lived for the community. A two-day absence cannot explain this.

Weeping, the woman picks up her firstborn's head, directs her steps to Musima's compound, a short distance away. There is not a living soul. The stench is horrendous. It smells not so much of death as of total annihilation. A death from which one can never be reborn. She inspects the huts one by one. All are deserted. In one, the disorder is indescribable: jars shattered, calabashes toppled, remains of meals scattered. Still holding her son's head, she skirts around the last hut, comes to the backyard. There lies Musima, flat on his stomach, his right hand clenched. Once again, she lets go of the head, wonders if she will have the strength to walk to the village square where the Council hut is located. She should still find the elders there. They could not have resolved the thorny question of interim leadership yet. She knows these men well. Most of them are ready to put their personal interests before the community's. The talks will take time.

With her heart pounding, the midwife discovers a territory emptied of its inhabitants. Here and there, family totems and utensils knocked to the ground bear witness to the ferocity of whatever struck the village. In front of some huts, lifeless bodies are starting to rot. Faces are contorted into masks of pain. Eyes are wide open, frozen with fear and incomprehension. Again, the midwife feels like she is travelling in another dimension. These scenes can only be visions. At the thought that even more unbearable visions will be shown to her if she runs away, Ebeise abandons the idea of turning back as she would like to do. It is not good to retreat in the face of trials. This is her punishment for having wanted to withdraw from the world, to turn her back on sorrow. She continues, trying, despite it all, not to let her eyes stray. She must reach the Council hut. To walk without looking left or right. The woman strains to think but her mind keeps coming back to the moment when she recognized the mutilated head of her child in her hands. All she sees are the hollow sockets, the perforated flesh, the torn skin.

It is quiet in front of the Council hut. None of the usual sounds of the elders arguing. Ebeise stays glued to the spot for a moment. She must go in. She hesitates, would like someone to hold her hand, to be there. She is suffocating. She pokes her head through the narrow door, nearly passes out. This is the source of the putrid smell that envelops the village. The stink is dizzying. There are no words in her language to describe what she sees there. She falls to her knees vomiting. She must leave the village, by hook or by crook. Go seek out Ebusi. Leave. First, she has to muster the strength to bury the deceased. Can two women manage to do this on their own? But there are not even two women left in the village. There in the hut where those whose sons had gone missing were gathered, there is but half a woman left.

Not even the sobs of the elder can shatter the silence. After a life spent bringing the children of her people into the world, her only recompense will be to bury all the dead. So be it. This she will do. And if she must carry Ebusi on her back to take her out of what was a village, she is ready to do so. It is not good to run away from trials, at the risk of having to face a more devastating one still. That is what she tells herself. When her eyes alight on the pile of ashes that used to be the relic sanctuary, Ebeise wonders where she will find the force to accomplish her duty, one last time.

End Times

Bana is in a state of extreme excitability. When the sun starts its journey across Sisi, the man will take Eyabe and him to the ocean shore. The man will not go all the way there, but he will lead them nearby. Hidden in the shadows, he will stand guard. The woman has shaved her head. For several days now, she and the child have kept out of sight, seldom leaving their host's miserable hut. Some of the people with shaven heads living there are not trustworthy. Some are ready to do anything to improve their daily lot. Informing on others proves to be a profitable option. The captives gathered in this sector of the Isedu village often feel guilty. They were captured with other members of their community but not traded. The men with hen feet did not want them. Because they were too ill or too rebellious, or because they were suicidal. Some of them, upon arrival in Isedu country, were not even offered as merchandise; the local dignitaries preferred keeping them in their service instead.

Some, like Mukudi, boarded the ship but fate brought them back ashore. Several times, the man thought of telling Eyabe everything. Explain why the others were gone when he was still here. Tell her what now attaches him to Isedu country, to this ocean that terrifies him as much as he needs it. He did not find the words to do so. This would hardly have calmed her. Quite the opposite. Ceaselessly reliving the moment when he found himself alone, he blames himself for his hunger strike and the physical weakness that came in its wake. That was why he could not break free like his brothers did. When the time of the ultimate pact came, he had failed them. Initiated together, they had gone through a second birth. The experience was so intense they did not separate once they returned to the village. The spiritual leader had told them to stay together as a group during the day, only separate in the evening to be with their families again. Intent as they were on holding onto the emotions they had felt in the forest sanctuary as long as possible, they had no difficulty obeying him.

His brothers and he were together the night of the great fire, when the Bwele trapped them in their nets. It was his fault they separated thereafter. From the start, his refusal to eat began to weaken the bonds between him and the others of his age. Whereas they were still hoping that a point would come when they could fight their assailants, he had already given up. No one had criticized him. When he did not eat, his brothers continued to leave him his ration. It was their way of speaking to him in the hunting shelters, guarded by their assailants, where they were held during the day. The few times he had taken in some food, it had been by force. The Bwele hunters, enraged by his behaviour, pried open his mouth, thrust roots or fruits down his throat. One day he had bitten the hand in his mouth, which earned him a beating. He recalls the painful look on his brothers' faces, the protests of old Mundene, unable to stand by and watch in silence. What good did his rebellion do him? He thought of it as a way of holding on to his dignity. Protesting against injustice. Not being an accomplice to the crime of which he was a victim. Nothing remains of these acts save the image of nine bodies being thrown overboard. A united ennead of young volunteers. When sleep overtakes him, this scene haunts his dreams. He hears the song his brothers sang, in the belly of the 'boat', to spread the word.

It was Mukate, Eyabe's son, who had started. His deep voice had filled the space, reached his companions. The men with hen feet had been careful to separate them. They were put one at a time by other captives in the bowels of the immense vessel. This way, they thought they would not be able to communicate, foment trouble. There were stories of prisoners who had managed to get their hands on powder kegs in the hold of the moving prison, had blown up the vessel sending the jailers and abducted alike to another world. Others, it was said, had put their tormentors to death, thinking they would get back ashore by their own means. But not knowing how to handle the ship, they were condemned to drifting endlessly over the waters. Onto madness. Onto death.

There was much talking among the prisoners with shaven heads. The man listened without taking part. He knew what happened to his brothers, had no desire to share it with anyone. It was his burden; it preyed on his mind at every moment of the six periods that divide the day of the living. It stalked him relentlessly. The singing. The bodies falling into the water. Old Mundene's raucous sobbing. And he. When all this was happening, he had been too weak to feel anything. He was aware of nothing but his physical handicap. The impossibility of concentrating. His body had dominated his mind. What an admission for a new initiate!

Haunted by these memories, the man asks himself what drove him not so much to refuse his fate as to single himself out to that degree. Why break the unity with his brothers? Why show no regard for the solidarity? What result could he have hoped for? Death did not mean extinction. The deceased simply lived in another dimension. Yes. Yet he could not ignore the truth. He had desired death as ardently as he had mainly because he wanted the ordeal to end. To suffer no more. The possibility of being reincarnated mattered little to him. Death, as he envisioned it, had to be an end. His brothers, on the other hand, kept on the side of life. Until the very end. There was something noble in their choice. The spiritual guide, hearing Mukate's sing, had warned them. He disapproved of their act but understood it. Lying on his back, the man's empty gaze roams over the branches that form the roof of his hut. The changing brightness of the sky is visible through the many gaps in the poorly assembled covering, so it is easy to measure the passage of time. This day seems interminable to him.

Watching Bana who is also examining the sky, attentive to the slightest variation, he says: *We have to speak to our mother.* The child turns around: *On the shore.* Eyabe pretends not to hear the exchange. She pictures again the moment she has been waiting for. After emptying the earth into the water, commending her son and his brothers to Nyambe, she will have to set out on the road quickly. She thinks of the journey that will take her back to Bebayedi. She will have to avoid the routes the captives took, which pass through Bwele country, find the way she came. The woman recalls the direction to take to reach the Kwa river. There she will wait for her ferrymen. She goes over the path in her mind, trying to remember details that will help her avoid erring. The tree split by lightning. The hunting shelter. What else? She is too anxious. She feels as if she has grown older since her departure, has travelled across ages. Her trip was not limited to covering the distance from one place to another. All of a sudden, she feels herself faltering. Only Bana, the child, will walk with her to the water's edge.

She sneaks a look at Bana. Initially she took him for a young boy, alone in the world, struck dumb by the horrors he had witnessed. But in reality no one knows anything about what he lived through or where he came from. They told her he had first appeared in the perimeter of Bebayedi country in the company of an old man who had not survived. They assumed they had left the same country together but they were not sure. It was not until they arrived in Isedu territory that Eyabe began wondering. Not that Bana has done anything odder than usual. He continues to eat as little as before, speaks only in cases of extreme necessity. It is their host's attitude to the child that makes her see things differently. The very first day of their arrival the man said, referring to Bana: *Mother, this one is a multitude.* She did not understand, did not question him. Would he have answered? Eyabe keeps turning these words over in her mind: *This one is a multitude.* The more they echo in her thoughts, the clearer becomes the connection with the name the child has given himself. He is *Bana*, not because he has absorbed the Mulongo language lessons she gave him but because there are more than one dwelling in his body. And they have come for her.

She lets the worn material she was examining slip from her now-trembling hands, tries to reason with herself. Thus far in their travels together, Bana has never behaved badly towards her. He has done nothing to indicate with any certainty that he is not a child like any other. What is he expecting to tell her when they reach the ocean? Why only there? The woman decides to put her trust in the maloba who have protected her until now. Twilight will eventually descend on the world. Then she will go down to the ocean, cast into it the earth she took from under the dikube where the placenta from her first birth was buried. Then what is meant to be will be. Sitting by the door, but out of sight so as not to attract attention, Bana scans the sky. Captives with shaven heads walk back and forth, feigning not to look inside the hut. The dwelling is at the back of the sector. It is the last one before the area where the Isedu nobility live near the ocean. You must have a good reason to walk around there. The man does not address a word to the other captives.

Eyabe drives away the unpleasant thoughts that threaten to creep into her mind. As she is about to lie down on the material that serves as a mat, she catches sight of a woman with a shaven head standing a few steps from the door and looking at her fixedly, then pointing at her. The unknown woman's gesture is slow. Her gaze locks with Eyabe's. Before Eyabe has time to realize what is happening, two Isedu men, no doubt from Prince Ibankoro's militia, storm into the hut. She does not hear their voices, only the sounds of the ocean she will never see. Her eyes seek out Bana. Where the child was sitting just a few seconds before, there is nothing but a puddle of water.

*

Twenty-seven bodies. There were twenty-seven of them. She buried them as best she could. No corner of the village was overlooked. She climbed up the hill to find nothing but the ruins of the chiefdom and the dwellings around it. She walked to the gates of the village where she found one of the guards. They had dealt him a blow on his head, no doubt to knock him out. His skull was broken. Only when she saw this body, after having covered every inch of the territory, did the old woman really understand. An attack. Of course. Nothing mystical. Nothing mysterious. Just the folly of men. Who were the assailants? In truth, the question did not occupy her mind for long. Let them come back if they so desire. What more could they do? Days passed, nights too, without knowing which came before which, which gave birth to the others, which would prevail in the end.

Lost deep within herself, Ebusi could be of no assistance. The midwife worked on her own. No one will ever tell future generations that a woman alone bore the task of entrusting the last of the Mulongo to the earth. No one will ever tell about these events, because the future is over. This people is no more. There will be no descendants. A final tomb was sealed today. In it were the remains of a worm-eaten newborn. As she was carrying out her task, Ebeise did all she could to drive away the question: *Where is your mother and the others?* The child was unrecognizable. If she had not found the body in that particular compound, she would not have known who it was. On the land that belonged to the Mulongo, death ceased to be a crossing, a passage between dimensions.

For the departed to come back among the living, to penetrate the bodies of pregnant women, they need a community. A community to chant their name, tell their story, remember their tastes, the sound of their laughter. People must think of them, leave them their portion of food after the evening meal. For those who died here, there will be nothing but earth. The graves are shallow. Ebeise did not have the strength to dig down deep enough. Sooner or later the ground itself will spew these bodies back out. The wind will sweep the remains of bones far away. Rainwater will carry off the rests, scattering them far and wide. No one will reclaim them. Should she stay here to watch over the graves? When the time comes, who will put her body into the ground? And who will take care of Ebusi whose spirit is wandering? Life is not an attractive thing. Life is the first obligation. Even after all these upheavals, Ebeise remains attached to the philosophy of her people. It is all she knows. She clings to it. They wanted to obliterate all of this. That is why they burnt the relic sanctuary.

The assailants, whoever they are, did their utmost to leave no stone unturned. And yet destiny wanted her to survive, with her memories. She must leave the place. First the midwife thinks of heading to Bwele country. She knows the way, even if she has not been there since her youth. That would be the simplest thing to do. She understands their language a little. They know that the Mulongo people existed. Yes, they would be a rampart against oblivion. The relations between the two communities have always been cordial. What would be more natural than to seek refuge among friends? The woman lets out a long sigh, thinking she has caught sight of a glimmer of light in the darkness. As quickly as possible, she hastens to the hut where Ebusi spends her days. It will not be easy to convince her to leave the hut where she has vowed to stay until her firstborn returns. She cannot possibly leave her there. No son will return to the village. The midwife thinks she knows what to say to persuade Ebusi to follow her.

As she is mentally preparing her words, something stops her in her tracks. The time she spent burying bodies nearly clouded her memory. Absorbed by her task, the rigorous gestures involved, she nearly forgot certain events. Suddenly she sees herself in Eleke's hut, the day she finally paid her a visit after the great fire. Her friend was in a bad way, but her clarity had not left her. And she had suggested that the Bwele knew something. Something about the twelve missing men. The midwife feels a cold rage taking hold of her body from head to toe. A rage combining a grasp of the facts with full knowledge of her impotence. She remembers hearing the name Bwele on the lips of her dying friend. They were the last words she uttered. The motives of the assailants may still be unknown to her but the woman is now sure of their identity. She will have to lead Ebusi down a different road.

Maybe in walking to Jedu, they will find Mukano and his men. Maybe if they go that way they will see Eyabe. Maybe, by misfortune, they will encounter the Bwele warriors face to face. Whatever may be, they must leave. There is nothing left here any more.

*

It is not the main village square where the funeral ceremonies were held a few days ago. Here the ocean whispers in the earth's ear, caresses it languorously, relieves its thirst with froth-capped waves. Seeing it like this, it is hard for Eyabe to imagine it feeding on human bodies. And yet. Every fibre of her body cries out that this is it. Here lies the land of water. The grave from which rose the voice of her firstborn. What Bana had to say, she will not know. The militia that came to arrest her took her to the place of transactions between the Isedu dignitaries and the men with hen feet. In a circular area, facing the water, on stools laid out in a half-circle, sit seven Isedu notables. Facing them, a few feet away, are three foreigners from pongo, their backs to the ocean, with goods meant for exchange piled on mats.

The captives are lined up on the left, surrounded by Bwele hunters. On the right, stand the Isedu soldiers, properly armed. It was from this side that the woman was pushed forward by the prince's militia, so that she was immediately confronted by the impenetrable expressions on the faces of the chained captives. She often tried to picture this scene based on the accounts she heard from Mutimbo and then Mukudi. People in shackles, their heads shaven, stripped of their amulets and their finery. What was missing from their accounts, because it could not be conveyed, was the distress, the defeated looks on their faces. The looks of defiance too, looks that say that a day will come but that the night will be long. The accounts did not mention the swelling belly of a bound woman, the posture of boys not yet circumcised. Their words could not suffice for her to picture the chains. It is the first time she has seen such a thing. Little does it matter that she knows that the boys taken captive from Mulongo country are no longer alive; she still finds herself examining the faces of each of the captives in the mad hope of recognizing someone. They are not here, yet they are the ones she sees. This suffering was inflicted upon them. Arms hanging by her sides, short of breath, she wonders why.

Her eyes sweep over the items piled up on the mats at the foot of the foreigners. A heap of metal bars, objects apparently in wood that she imagines must be the fire-spitting weapons, bracelets, also in metal, shinier than the bars. How many do you need for a child? How many for a man? Are the pregnant women worth more than the others? What can be exchanged to pay for the affliction of the abducted, of those that will never see them again? Will it all end when the Isedu have taken over Bwele territory? Eyabe trembles at the thought that her clan's sons were forcibly dragged here. Their unexplained disappearance shattered the harmony of community life. No one will tell the Mulongo the destiny of their children. She surely will not, since she has been discovered. They will never know. They will continue to be suspicious of one another, to look for guilty parties to punish in their midst. Now is no longer the time to wonder about the silence of the ngambi, consulted in vain.

It is too late to try to decipher the message from the maloba, the signs sent by Nyambe. They alone know why the world had to come to an end, what reality will be born from its dissolution. One of the men who arrested her shouts a command at her. Seeing her wide-eyed incomprehension, he forces her to kneel and with his hand on her neck, tries to coerce her to bow her head. She resists without a sound. Eyabe fixes the high-ranking people with a defiant look. Ibankoro, whom she recognizes by his head-covering rimmed in luminous thread and the abundance of necklaces over his torso; Njole, whom she had seen on the main square during the funeral. Other dignitaries are present. The only face she does not seek is Mutango's.

Since she still has not bowed her head, the soldier strikes her. She falls face down, decides not to talk. She has nothing to say to any one of them. The men with hen feet seem embarrassed by this incident which interrupts their business. Yet they voice no objection. The woman thinks of Mukudi who was taken to the white building. She also sees the face of the woman who denounced them. It does not move her. Her mind has soared far away. The prickly sensation of the sand against her skin leaves her indifferent. She barely hears the Bwele notable speaking in Mulongo: *Woman*, he says, *your scarifications betrayed you. Your shaven head will fool no one. What are you doing here?* Eyabe does not reply. Her silence carries more words than she could utter. It booms more powerfully than a drum, thunders more loudly than fire-spitting weapons.

Princess Njolę breaks the silence. There is a laugh in her voice, though not in the voice of the man translating what she says: *You can keep your reasons to yourself. The Mulongo are now our people. Believe me, we will know how to teach them to walk straight. The twelve we caught the first time caused a great disturbance. They made us lose face. But the affront has been expunged. You should know that your words are nothing to me.* Turning to the man who is standing on her right, she adds a few words. He hastens to transmit them: *We will discuss your fate. Either you will be taken to one of our regions where people from your clan are grouped together or we will keep you here where His Highness Ibankoro will do with you as he likes. After all, it is his territory that you violated.*

The Isedu prince informs the assembly that he has no interest in this woman. The last people of her clan to have set foot in this territory were a source of trouble. Once again he had to deliver hostages to the foreigners to compensate for the nine captives. Only an old, practically useless man remained, and another who is in a pathetic state. From him too, there is nothing to be gained. *Since they are your people,* he adds, *I am counting on our sister Njanjo and you to make them more . . . compliant. Otherwise, our agreements will not hold. To produce captives to trade, I will apply the old tried-and-true methods.*

Njolę does not respond right away. With a wave of her hand she summons her servant to fan her more vigorously, sends for something to drink. From where she is, Eyabę thinks she hears the Bwele princess swallowing. Her voice reaches her like a buzzing when she speaks again: *Brother, you yourself will admit that what happened was unforeseeable. What I mean is that occult forces were put into play. The one to blame was surely the old sorcerer. Capturing him was a mistake but he was with the young initiates when our hunters caught them. He can do nothing any more since 'the ship' has taken him away.* Finally, she regards the loss of the Mulongo men as a blessing in disguise. It was what made Queen Njanjo decide to strike a fatal blow to this community. It was a major operation, proof that the Bwele did not take the incident lightly.

To capture an entire clan, men had to be deployed through the bush for several days. Luckily, the Mulongo seldom went out. They were busy with communal rituals prior to the departure of their chief. This helped greatly in setting up the operation. Henceforth landless, deprived of their Minister of Rites and of their chief, the Mulongo will be the most compliant captives they have known. Scattered across the vast Bwele territory, they will soon stop speaking their language, will never be able to recreate the cohesion of their group whose very name will disappear. Absorbed by the Bwele, from now on they will form a cast of submissive individuals, good for trading. It is no mean accomplishment to have succeeded in doing this without embarking on a war with them.

The Bwele notable deliberately translates his princess' words, hoping to elicit a reaction from Eyabe. The woman listens distractedly to all this chatter. Her attention is now wholly focused on the ocean. She saw it when Ibankoro soldiers took her to their sovereign. Here, she hears it, as she had not until then. The voice of her firstborn is in the roaring waters. He is lamenting the peace he will never be granted. Eyabe thinks about the jar of earth she left in the hut. She took such care of it, hugging it to her body nearly all the time. At night she used it as a headrest, a vehicle for her dreams to carry her to days gone by. Love. Shared joys. She would have liked so much at this very moment to hold a fistful of earth from that container. Throw it into the water before hurling herself in. Too bad. It will be her own body that she will offer up to the waves to put an end to the torment of the unburied dead. May they be at peace, even if they cannot be reborn. The woman leaps to her feet, takes flight, races with all her might to the ocean.

*

They walk side by side, pressed tightly against one another, advancing with small steps to jedu. The vegetation keeps them from going faster. They did not take a cutlass, to cut the unruly branches. No matter, they have all the time in the world. When you do not know where you are going, there is no need to rush. The older woman carries the satchel with what they need for sustenance. They did not take much. They are not hungry. When night falls, they stop walking, pray for assistance in their trials, surrender to sleep.

Fear is beside the point. What is there to worry about when all has been lost? On the way, they may encounter an animal, an ill-intentioned person, a bad spirit. They are not apprehensive. One of the women is thinking of nothing but finding her son. That is the reason she agreed to leave the village. The elder told her it was the only way. *We are going in the direction of jedu, in the footsteps of our janea. By now he must have news of Mukudi. Come, let us go.*

The matriarch lied. She had no choice. Ebusi would not have come otherwise. She would have stayed where she was with her hands over her ears, the name of her firstborn on her lips. The old woman does not know whether her companion will survive the trip. She is so weak after the many days without eating. She has not washed since she moved into the communal hut, which makes the stench from her body hard to bear. This, though, does not sway Ebeise from her purpose. The smell was nearly sweet compared to the putrid stink of the decomposing bodies she had to clean before burying them in graves so shallow the earth would not keep them long. These cadavers will not replenish the land. The plants will not draw sustenance from them. From every point of view, these are useless deaths. Aberrant deaths.

Ultimately, what she told her companion had not been a complete lie. She is doing her best to follow the path the chief must have taken. Without letting her hopes soar too high in her heart, the woman who was for long the midwife of the Mulongo would like to be allowed to see individuals from her village still alive before leaving for the other world. To be given the chance to tell them about the horror. It is impossible to see all this and be silent. She cannot talk to the travel companion about it because Ebusi hears nothing at all—unless her son's name is pronounced. All that the elder asks is not to leave this world with all this pain inside her. It is already dreadful to imagine that her spirit will no longer have a community to watch over. She rejected, not so long ago, the mere idea of reincarnating to live once again on earth.

Now the prospect of one day being a spirit with no attachments almost drives her to tears. But if she cries, she will collapse, she will not be able to get a hold of herself. Instead, she thinks. Mulls over the same questions again and again. If it was indeed the Bwele who did this, what did they do with the people whose bodies she did not find? What did they do with the twelve men who disappeared the night of the great fire? And, especially, why? There never were any difficulties between the two populations. If the Bwele had needed anything at all, their neighbours would have taken it upon themselves as their duty to help them. They would have felt honoured to do so. The elder wonders whether her people, no doubt moved by their past, lived too cloistered from the world. Having had to run from their own brothers, the children of Emene carried the wounds of the exodus, then the exile. They believed they were safeguarding themselves by not venturing out to explore the world. Perhaps they would have found allies. They never again uttered the name of the country whence they came, never returned to it to make peace. To say: *Generations have gone by but we are still your flesh and blood. Let us know each other.*

They alone could have done this, since Muduru's descendants did not know where to find Emene's. But the Mulongo never retraced their steps in the opposite direction, from mikondo to pongo, to tread once again on the land of their origins. The clan lived as if it had given birth to itself. Terrorized by violence, it ritualized and regulated it, so as to resolve conflict with words. Mukano embodied this philosophy to perfection. Did he do wrong? She does not think so. Yet, she cannot help but recognize the dangers of such thinking when one must share the world with other people who see life differently. Without much conviction, Ebeise says to herself that her husband Mundene could have protected the clan. She recalls the early days of their life together when he told her the community's secret history, the mystical version of the Mulongo story. In the days of Emene, the founder of the clan, the Minister of Rites was powerful enough to make the entire community disappear. Thus, predators, human or animal, could not see the people who followed the queen. This is how they managed to walk for such a long time, from pongo to mikondo, and only stop when the soles of their feet wedded the ground.

Mundene, who confided many things to her, never went so far as to disclose the secrets of his practice. She did not know if he had the ability to remove an entire village from the sight of potential assailants. Of course, to do so, he would have had to know in advance that there was a threat. The spiritual guide by Queen Emene's side did not need to ask the ngambi to know that malicious forces were at work in the known world, and even beyond. Being compelled to leave her home, to rush headlong into the unknown, even at the risk of death, required precautions. It was not the same for the Mulongo. The clan had found a haven of peace, had huddled inside it. Mundene, like the rest of the community, had been taken by surprise by the great fire, had not suspected its origin. Now he was gone. The village too. Eleke's visions proved to be too vague to show them the way. Stunned by his new responsibilities, Musima too had not known what to do. Death had struck him down as he was trying, once again, to get the ngambi to speak. Had the ancestors remained deaf to his calls or was it he who had failed? No one will ever know. They should have kept their eyes open to the visible world, that is all she knows.

What would she say to the janea, she who so wanted to see him again? If they were to meet, their reunion would be more a source of sorrow than of consolation. Mukano's heart would burst asunder. He would want to see with his own eyes what had befallen the land of his predecessors, what remained of the people for which he was responsible. He would lay his eyes on the relic sanctuary, now a mound of ashes. Climbing the hill where the chiefdom once stood, he would behold the carbonized ruins. His cries of rage would echo in a vacuum. He would suffocate, crushed by the reek of death hanging over the land. Then he would remember his visit to the Bwele queen, would know that Njanjo had lied to him when she pretended to know nothing of the lost Mulongo men. He would understand that she purposefully misled him, sent her hunters to attack the village. He would want to confront her. Ready to declare war for the first time in the history of his people. Mukano would realize that the only warriors left were the eight men of his personal guards. Even a child would not think of braving the Bwele with so few fighters.

Unquestionably, it would be a painful reunion. Yet this very prospect is what keeps Ebeise from collapsing right there, waiting for the end to come. She refuses to give in. Everything around her was destroyed but she was spared. There must be a reason. As they walk, she listens to her companion who is humming a nursery rhyme, clapping her hands in time, rocking an imaginary new-born in her arms. And this woman? Were it given to her to find her firstborn and thereby recover her senses, how could she stand the disappearance of her other children? It is better for her to stay lost in her memories, to have eyes only for happy days. The elder puts her arm around Ebusi's shoulders, draws her close. The woman laughs. The laughter of a little girl. She does not notice that the two have reached a swampy area. It is impossible to take another step. Ebeise looks at the mud that comes up to her calves. There is a smell here that resembles the stench that spread over the village they left behind. The old woman turns around and realizes they cannot retrace their steps to find another way.

Caught in this slimy mire, they can barely move their toes. Solid ground is nowhere to be seen. Nothing around them indicates the presence of people, of someone who could hear them if they cried out for help. They must not wear themselves out in pointless shouting, must not sink down into this foul-smelling bog. Ebeise imagines with horror what it would be like to let herself be submerged by this substance, to feel it enter her nose and mouth. Ebusi, having just noticed the strange texture of the ground, seems tempted to sink her hands into it. The elder woman feels incapable of holding her back for long. She looks around for a branch, a stick, even a liana, anything they can lean on or hang onto. In the tangle of adventitious roots of a shrub whose name she does not know, the woman who is no longer the midwife of the Mulongo discerns an object. She narrows her eyes to see better.

Tears fill her eyes at the sight of one of Chief Mukano's mbondi. Then he and his men came this far. Did they go further? Did this sticky silt get the better of them? No. There were nine of them. Mukano and eight of his soldiers. She wants to believe they managed to extricate themselves from it. Without moving, the woman focuses her attention on the shoes: a piece of leather, fashioned by the clan's best artisans. The janea must have lost it because of the sludge. Where can he be? There is no one. The branches of these shrubs are too flimsy to bear the weight of anyone seeking protection from the muck. Ebeise is too tired to let herself be overcome by panic. Although it may not be reason enough, the mere fact of seeing an object not far away that belonged to Mukano prompts her desire to reach the shrubbery. She has no idea what she will do when she does so, but it is as good an objective as any. With Ebusi by her side, having a goal, no matter how modest, is the only thing to do. Keep moving. If night finds them there, Ebusi will want to sit or lie down. The old woman is in no rush to see what would happen. If she must admit defeat, she will have tried everything possible beforehand.

Holding Ebusi firmly against her, the matriarch focuses on her feet, trying with all her might to lift one, at least one, from the mud that is sucking her in. Laughing hilariously, her companion surrenders to the embrace like a child, so that all the efforts fall on the midwife's shoulders. Ebeise begins singing to boost her courage, a joyless melody, like those that the women of her clan composed to express the darkness of the great fire, the disappearance of their loved ones, the reclusion of ten suffering mothers in an isolated hut. The song she is singing is made to be joined by other voices. It recounts what she knows of the final days of the Mulongo clan, names the people who went missing after the great fire, calls by name the women whose sons disappeared, recalls their first birth. She remembers Eleke, who was closer than a sister to her. *One of us,* she says, *had to go wait for the other in the land of the dead.* She thinks of her eldest son, whose head she had to pull away from a hen. She thinks of her husband, the master of mysteries, who did not manifest himself. She convokes the chief, questions the sages of the community whom she had to bury.

Her legs are growing numb. She does not let go of Ebusi or abandon her efforts. She feels she may have succeeded in moving her right foot a little. Then she hears a voice. Someone is singing with her, marrying the rhythm of her improvised lament, instinctively finding the missing phrases to punctuate the refrains. It is in Mulongo that a woman accompanies her, saying: *Eee, our aunt, this I have been told. Eee, our aunt, and much more.* Ebeise falls silent, listens attentively. She recognizes the voice, at least thinks she has, but she has to see the woman's face to be sure. Then she will know if it is a malevolent spirit playing tricks. What she sees between the branches of shrubs a few steps away, not far from the place she is trying to reach, is not a familiar figure. Only a silent little girl. An unknown child, perched on a tree trunk, staring at her. The child stretches out her arm. For a moment, Ebeise sees nothing but this arm. The other voice repeats: *Eee, our aunt, this I have been told. Eee, our aunt, and much more.* It is only for this reason that the midwife ends up looking in the direction to which the child is pointing. There she recognizes Eyabe.

*

The people who live behind these swamps came to help them. It took them time to pull the midwife's massive body out of the mud. They took the two women to their rafts on the banks of a river that they call Kwa, which means justice in their language. The women of the community made them welcome. They lived in the hut reserved for newcomers. There, they were surprised to find Musinga, Eyabe̱'s husband and the janea's designated investigator. He had set out in the direction of jedu, following his sovereign, well after the departure of the latter. He was worried. The Council proved to be incapable of administering the community. He had reached the marsh the evening before the men of Bebayedi discovered the lifeless body of Mukano. They have been treating him since then for a fever he contracted the night he spent stuck in the bog, surrounded by decomposing corpses. His condition improved when Eyabe̱ returned. When he saw her, he murmured: *With a little training, you would make an excellent tracker.* In a solemn tone she asked: *Why did you not come to see me in the communal hut? Did you too think that I had killed our son?* The man shook his head in denial. Not only had he never thought so but he had also discreetly come to the hut nearly every day. *It was impossible to approach you directly, but I never abandoned you. Do you not know me better than that?*

While the midwife and her companion were resting, the woman who had gone in search of the land of water told the story of her travels. Yes, the land of water exists. It stretches from the coast to the horizon. You cannot travel over it by foot, neither can you measure its expanse. It is said that lands exist beyond it, inhabited by human beings. The foreigners with hen feet are thought to come from one of these faraway shores. Eyabe described everything she saw, heard and felt since she left the village. She omitted no detail, not even the mystery of her death and her rebirth. The old woman and Ebusi learnt that, seeing no more honourable solution, she had thrown herself into the ocean. They have difficulty picturing this aquatic space, when a river is already a remarkable phenomenon to them. They have no idea what an ocean could possibly mean, but they listened. They trembled, wept. Stifled cries, wept. Swore, wept, wept . . .

Eyabe described what happened under the water when she was drowning. Bana was there, as he could not show himself to be on the land of the living. He displayed his nine faces that spoke with one and the same voice: *When they took us into the belly of the boat, other captives were already there, from places we knew nothing of. They separated us so that there could be no united strategy. Mukate was the one who had the idea but we all agreed and followed him. He sang to us his proposal to abandon our bodies. In this way, we would return to the village, ask our mothers to give birth to us again. The Minister of Rites warned us against this plan. Leaving our bodies to avoid trials was forbidden. Should we have listened to him? Our mothers did not recognize us. By the time we tried to take back our bodies, the men with hen feet had thrown them into the water. That is why we are here. Only our brother Mukudi and the old Mundene stayed on the ship. It was crucial for someone to come. For us to be heard . . .*

Mundene had been taken away with the other captives. If he survived the crossing, he must now be in a territory situated on the other side of the ocean. If his spirit must span this whole expanse of water to manifest itself, it is not surprising that there has been no news from him. Mukudi was brought back ashore. He was in bad shape. The foreigners did not want him. They said they had been swindled. After she heard the words of the missing, Eyabe awoke in the white building on shore. The Isedu soldiers had dived in after her, heeding their sovereign's order. They saved her from drowning, though she resisted them. The shackled captives that were being traded there or the servants with shaven heads that might get wind of it must not be tempted to follow her example. She found herself in the jail with Mukudi, who had been put in isolation. There Mutango appeared in the middle of the night. The man, now in the service of the archer princess of the Bwele, had bribed the guards to let him in. Unable to speak, since his tongue had been cut out, he used gestures to explain that he would take the place of the woman. She could leave. No one would stop her. All they had to do was swap clothing. Thin as he had become, he could easily put on Eyabe's clothes, fool them until the return of the sun. When she would leave, they would mistake her for him. They had to hurry.

Eyabe turned to Mukudi, begged him to come with her. They would go together to wait for the ferrymen, settle near the marsh. Their people had been captured, taken away from their home. They had no village any more. There was no need for him to stay in Isedu country to remember his brothers. They did not reproach him for anything. They died hoping to have a chance to live again. To honour them he must accept that he had survived them. Thus, they had set out together on the road. This is the story the woman relates. Now Ebusi must understand why her first-born asks her not to call him Mukudi any more. He wants to be reborn in his way on the banks of the Kwa. What his brothers did not accomplish, he wants to realize in their name. Mother and son stand by the water. Children are throwing nets, trying to catch fish. The most talented do so with their bare hands. She asks: *Is that why you did not answer me? Because you do not want to bear this name any more?* He replies: *I did not hear you because it is no longer my name. The person you are speaking of died with the others. I myself do not know who I have become but we will discover it together if you help me.* Not very far away, Eyabe is talking with Ebeise. The matriarch listens attentively. She smiles, hearing Eleke's voice whispering in her ear: *Listen to her. Wherever she may go, this one is the daughter of Emene.*

The woman says this land is called Bebayedi. It is the country that those who escaped capture found for themselves. Here, the memories of the different peoples join to weave a story. The midwife asks what will

become of them without the help of the ancestors, without being able to recognize, on the ground, the marks of their passage. How can one move forward when others have not already paved the way. The woman answers that their forbearers are within them. They are in the drum rolls, in the way is prepared, in beliefs that endure and are transmitted. The people who came before them in the land of the living inhabit the language they are speaking. It will be transformed through contact with other languages that it will infuse as much as the others will permeate it. The ancestors are here. Neither time nor space limits them. They reside wherever their descendants are. *A great many of ours have perished*, she adds, *but not all are dead. Where they have been taken, they are doing as we do. Even in hushed tones, they speak our language. When they cannot speak, it remains the vehicle of their thoughts, the rhythm of their emotions.*

The woman says that you cannot dispossess people of what they have received, learnt, experienced. They themselves could not do so, even if they wanted to. Human beings are not empty calabashes. The ancestors are here. They float over bodies that embrace. They sing when lovers cry out in unison. They wait at the threshold of a hut where a woman is in labour. They are in the cry, the babble of newborns. *Little ones tell of the spheres they knew before being amongst us. If we could understand, we would know which old souls dwell in these new bodies. At times we do. We can see it if we are attentive.* Children grow up, learn the words of the earth, but the bond with the realms of the spirit lives on. The ancestors are here and they are not a confinement. They conceived a world. This is their most precious legacy: the obligation to invent in order to survive.

The woman says that the dead must be mourned. Nine boys from the clan left their bodies so that their spirits could return to their loved ones. In this new land of Bebayedi, a burial site will be made for them. Makube trunks will be buried in the ground. After nine moons, they will build a hut over these graves, with each supporting pillar bearing the name of one of the young deceased men. This will be the village sanctuary. An ennead of men perished seeking the lost sons of Mulongo. The bodies of Mukano and his guards rest in the marshland near Bebayedi. Torrential rains lasting several days took them by surprise. They drowned there. The people of this community, who had retreated to their huts to take shelter from the rain, were unable to help them. It was the smell that alerted them once the deluge had passed. The chief was caught in tanda roots. The upper part of his body was rotting in the sun.

In a single night, right after the discovery, flowers known as manganga began sprouting in abundance in this part of the marsh. Little by little, the water began bringing personal effects to the surface: the spears, the amulets of the Mulongo soldiers; the chief's mpondo, his mbondi imprisoned in the bog— the other having been found later by Ebeise—his ekongo and his staff of authority. All these things will be entrusted to the midwife, until the sanctuary is built. The woman says that twenty-seven people were buried in the land of yore. Their names will be transmitted here so that they will know that a people acknowledges them, claims them as its own. The matriarch nods her head. Out of fear of being misunderstood, she dares not say: *All is well.* So she whispers: *May we know how to welcome the day when it comes. The night too.*

Glossary of Douala Terms

Names of plants and trees are not translated as there is not always a known equivalent in French or English. Other notions are left in Douala for the same reason or when a translation seems unnecessary.

betambi (singular: etambi): sandals

dibato (plural: mabato): fabric

dindo: meal marking the end of a trial, prepared with unusual ingredients

elimbi: drum

Etina: a particular day of the week

eyobo: penis sheath

Inyi: female figure of God the Creator

iyo: mother

Kwasi: a particular day of the week

janea: chief

jedu: east

maloba (singular: loba): secondary divinities, manifested, for instance, in the elements

manjua: item of clothing with fringes, made of plant fibres and resembling a skirt; worn as a sign of mourning mao: palm wine

mbenge: west

mbua: rain

mbondi: short boots worn by the chief when he travels

mikondo: south

misipo: the universe

mpondo: royal cape in leopard skin

Mukosi: a particular day of the week

musuka: royal hairdo

Mwititi: darkness, shadow

ngambi: oracle

ngomo: drum

Nyambe: God the Creator

Nyangombe: divinity of sterility

pongo: north

sango: title given to men as a sign of respect, the equivalent of 'Mister' or 'Lord'

sanja: loincloth

Wase: the Earth

Acknowledgements

I want to thank Sandra Nkaké who, in September 2010, presented me with *La Mémoire de la capture*, a short report for UNESCO written by her mother, Lucie-Mami Noor Nkaké, and published in 1997. The purpose was to see if a memory of the transatlantic slave trade existed in sub-Saharan Africa. The investigation, conducted in south Benin with support from the Société africaine de culture and UNESCO, demonstrates the existence of an oral heritage on the subject and the relevance of carrying out further research, including in other sub-Saharan countries.

This report was not intended for a writer of fiction. No doubt many would regard such a document, often technical, as boring. Yet I found in it confirmation of very long-standing intuitions that, having become obsessional, run through and sustain my literary output.

Readers of my writings would not be surprised to learn that for years I have been perusing texts on the transatlantic slave trade and other subjects related to the experience of sub-Saharans and Afro-descendants. However, *Season of the Shadow* would not have seen the light of day in this form without *La Mémoire de la capture*, to a large extent because of the title given to the report. What memory do we have of the capture? Can we remember these uprootings without saying who the people were who experienced them and how they saw the world?

Describing the everyday life of the sub-Saharan communities who lived through the colonization necessitated research. To render these populations, it was important to acquire extensive knowledge of all aspects of their lives and their thinking. By pure chauvinism, I used as a basis my own cultural reference point—Central African Bantus, who are implicated in the transatlantic slave trade even though they seldom speak of it. As for the mythology, beliefs, clothing and so forth, *Season of the Shadow* owes much to the work of Prince Dika Akwa nya Bonambela, in particular to his *Les Descendants des pharaons à travers l'Afrique: la marche des nationalités kara ou ngala de l'antiquité à nos jours* [The Descendants of the Pharaohs across Africa: The March of the Kara or Ngala Nationalities from Antiquity to the Present Day (Brussells: Éditions Osiris-Africa, 1985)].

Last but certainly not least . . . my family.

For all the populations that are part of the narrative, the sub-Saharan language used in this book is Douala from Cameroon. It was sometimes necessary to fill the gaps in my linguistic knowledge.

I thank my mother, Chantal Kingué Tanga, for having answered all my questions about plants and for having searched for answers when she did not have them immediately available.

Thanks go to Philippe Nyambé Mouangué who provided me with precious and pivotal elements for writing this novel, especially with regard to the non-racial perception of Europeans that we had on our shores.